CITY OF RAINS

CITY OF RAINS

NIRMAL DASS

thistledown press

National Library of Canada Cataloguing in Publication Data

Dass, Nirmal███
City of rains / Nirmal Dass.

ISBN 1-894345-62-2

I. Title.
PS8557.A612C57 2003   C813'.6   C2003-911152-0

Cover photograph by Jeremy Maude/Masterfile
Cover and book design by J. Forrie
Typeset by Thisttledown Press

Thistledown Press Ltd.
633 Main Street
Saskatoon, Saskatchewan, S7H 0J8
www.thistledown.sk.ca

Thistledown Press gratefully acknowledges the financial assistance of the Canada Council for the Arts, the Saskatchewan Arts Board, and the Government of Canada through the Book Publishing Industry Development Program for its publishing program.

for Georgina:
So many journeys...

ACKNOWLEDGEMENT

My sincerest thanks to Seán Virgo, my editor —
deep-minded, keen of eye — a true *fili: ghrinn
fhuaránach fhorasda.*

The residue of faces, speech of sleeping hands:
some are no more, others forgotten,
in the bright rustle of dawn.

~~~

The heart is sorrow's eternal nest.

PEOPLE HERE THINK I'M A TOURIST, and no doubt I look like one with my camera and general bewilderment —and, of course, my "Americanized" French.

But while the tourists wander about, consulting their guidebooks, taking in all the historical sites — from the Middle Ages to the Nazi occupation — the history I am retracing is less than a lifespan away.

My guidebook is not *Michelin*, or *Lonely Planet*. It is a map of sorts — carefully written out, and I have followed it all day, since I stepped off the train from Paris this morning.

Sitting here, now, at my table on the terrasse of the Hotel Astrid, I wait for the day to end. When I savour the food they bring me, I taste with another man's tongue. When I raise a glass of the crisp apple brandy that is Normandy's pride and hallmark, I am searching in the bouquet for what another man found there.

And when a pretty girl walks by, with that gait that French women seem to be trained in from childhood, my head is the only one that doesn't swivel.

As dusk falls, the city of ghosts and secrets seems to draw closer. And in that other twilight of dawn I shall go out and walk down to the river, when no one is around. Oh, there will be delivery boys, and tradesmen, and the sleepy hookers of course (they are there in my map), but they will be occupied with their own affairs.

They will pay no attention to a solitary figure, down below Pont Guillaume le Conquérant, or wonder what he is doing as he kneels there beside the water. In this city where promises are broken as readily as hearts, how could they guess that I have crossed an ocean and traced the old streets of Rouen to honour a debt.

They could never imagine the journey that ends for me here — a journey that started in a little Himalayan village where fate once tossed me.

I HAD NEVER BEEN TO INDIA BEFORE, and I wasn't prepared for the assault. Perhaps it was a mistake to land in Bombay and then head north to New Delhi, but it was a mistake I had to live with.

The great wash of misery overwhelmed me; the hard-heartedness of the well-fed towards the starving revolted me. I had to get out.

After a two-week stay in that crowded, swarming capital, singed by the tactics of beggars, the vacant hopelessness of street-children's eyes — the shallow carelessness that fringes the heart of mystical India — I headed west, and then swung due north.

I was heading for the foothills of the Punjab. My family's roots lie along Afghanistan's southern border, and I remember my grandfather softly singing the Pashto and Persian songs he'd learned as a boy.

My head was full of myths my family had clung to, despite having left the Punjab for a couple of generations.

I think I was trying to put flesh and blood on those myths.

But the reality from which these myths emerged had long vanished. Gone were the straight-backed regiments, the heroic adventurers, the hunting expeditions, the lore of the warriors, the pride in the steel of a well-forged sword, the joy in feeling the smooth stock of a carbine — which was one's only true friend.

The reality that met me was more sordid — the petty grubbing for money, careless greed, and an utter blindness to the past, though that past lay all around, almost as oppressive as the heat.

It is to my parents' credit that they insisted my siblings and I learn Punjabi, despite our resistance. But now, in the unkempt city of Manali, when I opened my mouth, I got amused stares, if not outright ridicule. I was speaking a Punjabi last heard during the time of Rudyard Kipling. Not only that — people would ask me with distaste whether I was a Muslim, for the dialect I spoke was only heard in that part of the Punjab that now lies in Pakistan. Of course, they had nothing against Muslims, but . . .

I was a strange and exotic beast moving among them. The Punjab I sought existed nowhere but in my mind.

Summer was almost over. Perhaps, I thought, if I left the city and went north, I might find the real Punjab, still intact. The air, I knew, would be cleaner, cooler and fresher. From my hotel window I could see the distant foothills of the Himalayas, capped in snow, rugged, ancient, pristine. They seemed to beckon me.

I went looking for a taxi that would be willing to take me away from the city's jumble and out in the country, up towards the mountains.

And as luck would have it, the first taxi driver I asked turned out to be from one of the mountain villages. He was happy to accept my offer. His name was Prakash Chand. He was a Hindu, of the Dogra clan.

I got in beside him, rather than sit in the back. This was apparently unusual, but he said nothing. I wanted to talk, not just sit and stare at the scenery.

"Why did you come down here?" I asked.

He looked at me sideways.

I expected the usual comment about my quaint Punjabi, but what I got surprised me.

"I fell in love with a beautiful girl, but she was betrothed to another. So, one night I sneaked over to her parents' house, and carried her off, and brought her here to Manali. She's my wife now!"

He gave me a happy grin.

"Didn't her family give you a hard time?" In my grandfather's stories, such abductions led to vendettas, pursuits, the avenging of family honour.

"They haven't found me yet!" he grinned again.

"And was your wife in love with you as well?"

His eyes took on a faraway look.

"She says she would forsake God himself to be with me."

I smiled. This was the language of romance. Perhaps it did survive after all, the mythic Punjab of those childhood stories — with its robber barons who lived by the might of their sword-arm, who robbed only from the rich, and defended the poor, who lived and died by a rigid code of the warrior — to be fearless before all, except God.

The little white taxi drove higher and higher, winding through narrow mountain roads that looked more like trails, but which were built for two-way traffic — a fact harrowingly demonstrated again and again.

The higher we got, the closer I felt myself to the India of my mind. Far below were the dusty plains where I was an alien. But among these mountains, I was at home. Perhaps it was some vestigial memory of the Afghan borderlands, my family's ancient home, that was kicking in. I was happy at last; I had made the right decision

"Do you speak any Pashto?" I suddenly asked Prakash.

He laughed.

"What do you think I am, some sodomizing Pathan?"

Surprised, I could only laugh along with him at this wicked old slander.

But among these mountains, I was thinking about my grandfather's songs. I wished he had taught me some of them. I wished I had listened more closely…

The taxi was obviously not built for Himalayan excursions. We laboured up one steep incline after another, losing speed but somehow enduring. And then all at once we were looking down on a deep green valley, mottled with fields of yellow and bright purple — the fabled saffron-bearing crocuses.

I gasped with delight. It was a Shangri-La. I was mesmerized.

"Let's go down there," I said.

Prakash gave me a quizzical look.

"Why?" he asked.

I merely repeated myself.

"Let's just go down there?"

"You're the boss," he said under his breath.

As we turned off, following a perilously steep grade, I understood his uneasiness. The taxi screeched and protested with its whole being. Prakash shoved it into the lowest gear. The car jerked hard, but still we were picking up speed.

We were halfway down, when I heard Prakash utter something I didn't understand.

This was followed by a stream of florid swearing.

"What's going on?" I found myself yelling, for the taxi began to swerve, and Prakash was having a hard time controlling the steering wheel.

A couple of times we glanced off the metal barrier that separated us from a two hundred-foot drop.

"The brakes! The brakes!" shouted Prakash. "They're gone!"

It's true what they say. Everything does happen in slow motion in a car crash.

We were nearly at the bottom of the grade, but the worst was yet to come.

A horse-drawn cart appeared out of nowhere.

Prakash pulled the steering wheel hard to the right.

The metal of the car groaned miserably. My hands pushed against the dashboard in an effort to brace myself. No seat belts, of course

Prakash leaned into the steering wheel; his face was slick with sweat and fear.

This was not a good move.

I heard something snap.

Prakash swore mightily again.

The steering wheel had come off.

"Jump out! Jump out!" He screamed, without looking at me.

He opened his door; mine was jammed.

I struggled and fought to get out.

Prakash did not wait.

He bailed out.

I heard him scream with pain as he hit the ground.

I gave up on the door, and braced myself again.

The car was heading straight for a brick wall.

In front of it, on a wooden cot, sat an old man, looking ever so serene, dressed in a white *kurta*-tunic.

"Get out of the way!" I shouted out, as if he would hear me.

The old man leaped up and away.

I shut my eyes tight and felt myself being hurled savagely forward.

The car stopped.

I opened my eyes.

The hood of the car looked like a squashed cigarette.

Acrid, pale smoke billowed up.

I tried to move.

I was caught in the shattered remains of the dashboard.

My door still wouldn't budge.

On the driver's side, the door had wrenched right off. Somehow I crawled across and out.

The cool air hit my face like a slap.

I was lying face down in tall grass.

I remember a green beetle scurrying close to my nose. I tried to turn my face away, but couldn't.

Then I felt someone pull me up, turn me over, and bend me in a sitting position.

I looked up.

It was the old man in the white *kurta*-tunic.

He was holding a glass of water to my lips.

I drank some.

He splashed the rest on my face.

The water was ice cold; it revived me.

"Thank you," I managed to mutter.

The old man smiled kindly. I thought he looked like my grandfather.

"*Mehrbane,* Thank you," I said again in Pashto, as I would to my grandfather.

His smile widened.

"*Ta poke-dalay shey?* Can you understand?" He asked with surprise.

"*Ze pohe-gam,* I understand," I said, trying to get up.

His hands steadied me.

"*Har tse sam dee!* Everything is alright!" He said as I struggled up.

His voice was deep and resonant — and his eyes were merry and deep blue — just like my grandfather's.

Was I dreaming? Was I in shock?

I looked at him again.

He smiled to encourage me.

Then his eyes twinkled merrily, mischievously.

"Welcome to Dhanoa!" He announced in an important voice.

Despite everything, I laughed.

Something my grandfather would have uttered, who said we had to laugh in the face of adversity.

And so, here we were, the old man and I, laughing away, while the car started sizzling behind us, and then burst into roaring flames.

CHAPTER 2

SOON THERE WAS A CROWD OF VILLAGERS standing around looking at me, and at the smoldering wreckage of Prakash's taxi.

The old man slid his arm around me and helped me to my feet.

I winced in pain. I could scarcely put any weight on my right foot.

I leaned heavily upon the old man, who bore me up without difficulty.

Slowly we headed for a clump of houses beside some tall poplar trees.

"You're young. You'll mend quickly," he assured me.

I nodded, though the pain was shooting up my leg. Then I remembered Prakesh.

"The driver . . . "

"Don't worry. He's alright. Just a bit of blood." The old man pointed to our left.

I saw Prakash being helped away by two men; someone had bound his head in a makeshift bandage.

The old man brought me to a little daub-and-wattle house, with a walled-in courtyard where a broad mulberry tree threw its shade.

He helped me lie down on a narrow wooden cot, wedged close to the trunk of the tree.

"You just rest here, and I'll get the teacher sahib. Now, don't wander off herding goats. Or should I tie a bell around your neck?"

He let out a hearty laugh, and disappeared through the front door.

I lay back and tried to master my pain; my ankle and leg were throbbing wildly.

I can't remember how long I lay there. Not long, I suppose.

Loud whispers and a few giggles came from the front door.

I propped myself on my elbow to get a better view.

The doorway was jammed with the eager faces of children; some of them serious, some of them laughing in their hands; all of them curious as hell to get a look at me.

I saw the children part. Their faces suddenly filled with awe.

As if at a signal, they scattered and were gone.

A tall, middle-aged man entered the courtyard, simply dressed in a *kurta*-tunic and a pair of pajamas, with short hair that hadn't yet begun to grey, and a close-cropped beard. He walked with a quiet confidence.

Following him was a small band of villagers, who stood back at a distance and showed the greatest deference to this strong-faced man.

He came over to the cot and carefully sat on one edge. His eyes were green, a colour often found in the Punjab. Once again, I found myself thinking of my grandfather.

"My name is Raj Kumar, and this is my house." His voice was low and soft.

"I've asked the doctor to come," he told me. "He'll be here soon. Of course, you're welcome to stay as long as you like. And don't worry about the taxi driver. He only gashed his forehead; nothing serious at all. You two were very lucky."

He patted my shoulder and rose.

The band of villagers looked to him for direction.

He spoke to them kindly, gently, as equals; there was no harshness in his voice, as I had heard being used by the people in Bombay or Manali whenever they spoke to someone they considered inferior.

"If I need anything, I'll let you know," he told the villagers, as he went into the house.

The band of men left the courtyard one-by-one, nodding goodbye to me.

Raj reappeared bearing a tube pillow in one hand, and a glass of milk in the other.

The pillow he carefully slipped under my ankle, which had swollen to twice its normal size. And he offered me the glass.

"Thank you," I said.

I again lifted myself on my elbow and sipped the cool fullness of the milk.

Raj said nothing more, but his demeanor put me at ease. And in the weeks that followed I never once felt that I was imposing on his goodwill.

I must have dozed off in the cool shade of the mulberry tree, because when I awoke, there was a short, stout mustached man carefully examining my ankle.

When I opened my eyes, he looked up and smiled.

"I'm Doctor Hari Lall. You've had quite an adventure, I hear." He had the same impish manner as the old man who had brought me here. Was this, perhaps, a Punjabi characteristic I was unfamiliar with?

He probed and prodded my ankle, and then very slowly rotated my foot.

That didn't hurt, and I told the doctor so.

He nodded with satisfaction.

"I don't think it's a fracture, and it's certainly not broken. It's a bad sprain, and if you stay off your feet for a few days you should be on the road to recovery." He opened his black bag and produced a roll of cotton bandages. "But why don't you come to my clinic in a day or two, and we'll do an x-ray, just to make sure."

I readily agreed. It was a relief, despite the pain, to know the damage was minor. And somehow in this little courtyard, with the leaves of the tree whispering above me, I was feeling something like peace.

After binding my ankle tight, the doctor closed up his bag, slapped both his knees, and rose.

I hadn't noticed but all this occurred while Raj was standing nearby watching.

He came forward and put his hand on the doctor's shoulder. "Thank you Hari for coming at a moment's notice."

The doctor gave a short laugh and slapped Raj's back exuberantly.

"I'm a doctor. What else am I good for?"

I called out. "Doctor, I haven't paid you yet. Wait." I fumbled about in my pocket, trying to fish out my wallet.

But the two men didn't hear me and walked out of the courtyard.

I lay back down, a little perplexed.

I heard them laugh a few times outside, and then I heard a car engine rev up, and the quick grind of gears.

Raj reappeared.

"I didn't pay the doctor."

Raj held up a hand, almost sternly.

"Don't you know it's impolite to talk about money? Payments are made quietly. You speak with a funny accent, by the way. I know you're not a native Punjabi. Where are you from?"

It was this little question that was the beginning of our friendship.

"I'm a Canadian," I replied.

He went into his room and returned with a little chair, and sat next to me.

"Canada," he said softly, "that's the country which defines itself as a mosaic of some kind."

"That is the theory," I said, "as opposed to the melting pot of America."

Raj looked at me and smiled.

"I think we're falling into clichés. But tell me this, if Canada is a mosaic, what picture do you see when the final piece is fitted in? And why is it that Canada is the only country in the world that has an identity problem?"

I had no answer.

His green eyes glinted with mirth. "No offence intended. It's just my way of talking, as you will discover."

He got to his feet. He was a tall and well-built man. "Well, I had better look after supper, since you'll be my guest."

"Are you sure?" I protested. "I don't wish to be a burden."

"When you start imposing," he said, "I'll let you know."

With that he picked up his chair and returned it to his room.

It took nearly a week before I could stand on my feet again, and then, at the end of his weekly visit the doctor drove me down to his clinic in Manali. Driving with him was a different experience — he drove expertly, casually, and his car had more power than that little white taxi. My nervousness vanished after the first hairpin bend.

His diagnosis was right. There was nothing broken or cracked. Before he drove me back, I left money beneath a piece of paper on his desk, when he wasn't looking.

My accident happened in late September, when the first crop of wheat is harvested and the winter crop seeded.

The rhythm of village life was slowly becoming my own, and I was getting familiar with my kind host.

The house Raj lived in was much simpler than I had imagined. It stood by the bright green wheat-fields, around which were smaller squares of crocuses that swayed purple in the breeze. It was these that I had seen as a patchwork from high up in the mountains. Near his house was a deep, rushing stream, fed by the melting snows of the Himalayas beyond. Its water was clear and cold. The villagers called it the "Piplan Nadi," or "Stream of the Poplars," because these trees grew tall along its banks.

In the courtyard, stood the little kitchen with its pile of wood and coal. And on the other side, behind a brick alcove, was the bathroom, containing only a much dented tin bucket and a small can.

The daily ritual consisted of filling the bucket with fresh water from the stream and scrubbing oneself clean with a bit of soap. No house in the village had a toilet; that job was done in the fields, at night or early in the morning before the bath.

There was a rhythm to Raj's life as well. He could be found in the evenings sitting on his cot, or his little chair, with the nightingales beginning their song in the mulberry tree.

Because he lived outside the village, there was no electricity in his house; at night from a distance a warm orange glow from an oil lamp could be seen slowly quivering upon the far wall of his bedroom.

No one could tell me about his past, and he spoke of it little; what I know I learned much later.

He earned his living teaching the village children. His wages arrived daily or weekly in the form of fresh-churned buttermilk, ground wheat still warm from the stone quern that women used to grind a daily supply for bread, large dollops of butter kept cool in a bowl of water from the stream, and basketfuls of vegetables and fruits in their season. It seemed to me, his life was enviably unfettered by modern complications.

The children came to their teacher in the morning, usually about nine o'clock, and stayed until noon; they gathered beneath the dome of the old walnut tree, eager-faced, it seemed to me, happy, bright-eyed.

This walnut tree stood on the far side of the stream, and was reached by crossing an unsteady rope bridge secured on both ends by large pegs. In the morning, among its thick, shiny leaves, countless birds added their songs to the voices of children beneath, reciting their lessons.

I decided that my idyll had come to an end, and it was time to go higher into the mountains.

I mentioned this to Raj later that evening.

He observed that I still walked with a pronounced limp, and perhaps it was better to stay a bit longer.

I did object and again brought up the subject of me being a burden and imposing on his hospitality.

"Is that how things are in Canada?" he asked me with a smile.

I didn't know what to say.

"Don't leave just because you think you've outstayed your welcome, because you haven't. Why not stay longer?"

How could I refuse? I agreed.

And then as an afterthought he added, "You remind me of what I was like in my younger years. I, too, never knew where I was going, or why. Stay, and maybe you can gather bits of life here that you can reminisce over in later years like old photographs."

"Is that what you do now?" I asked, and hoped that this didn't sound sarcastic.

"Perhaps it is." His voice had a sadness that I hadn't heard before.

And so, my few days in Dhanoa stretched into a month. In that poor mountain village, I recouped more spiritually than physically.

I learned about many things there — chief among them the realization that happiness can be found in the smallest of things, and that true friendship, no matter how brief, can last well beyond a lifetime.

During that month I learned to live frugally, speak softly, and to follow a regimen that carried me along from one day to the next. What once would have seemed mundane and monotonous, became a whole way of being.

One clear night, as we sat beneath Raj's mulberry tree, listening to the crickets play counterpoint to the nightingales, I asked him why it was he lived here in Dhanoa, alone. He answered with silence; I fell into silence, too.

But the next morning, as he got ready to leave for the walnut tree school, he handed me a red-covered journal.

"Maybe you'll find the answer to your question of last night in here."

There was that same sadness in his voice that I'd noticed earlier.

A faded little sticker on the cover roused my curiosity. It read *15F00.*

"Where did you pick up this journal?"

"In France, actually," he said in a matter-of-fact tone. "I lived there for many years. I am also a French citizen."

I looked at him with new eyes.

"You speak French, I presume, since you're from Canada?" Raj was smiling again; the sadness had vanished.

"A little, though not everyone from Canada does." My French was what I had picked up in high school, in my supposedly bilingual country — I could manage as long as I didn't have to speak it.

"Good, then you should be fine."

Soon I heard the voices of the children across the stream, diligently repeating their lessons.

And above their voices cooed the ever-present ringdoves that called the old walnut tree home.

CHAPTER 3

BEHIND RAJ'S HOUSE STOOD A GROVE OF APRICOT TREES all neatly pollarded. They rose straight and strong like a rampart of sweet-scented shade. They weren't planted in order but grew in a large copse; perhaps they were once wild and had been brought under cultivation.

The grass beneath these trees was soft and the breeze almost always cool.

With the journal Raj had given me in my hand, I made my way over to this grove.

It was a bright morning, and the few clouds above me changed shape with each lash of the wind.

As I sat down, a sudden hissing and honking swirled above me.

A willowy skein of Demoiselle cranes careened above the cropped heads of the apricot trees — long legs level with tails, wide black-fringed, grey wings held rigid, and blue, crested heads.

This was my first sighting. Soon there would be flocks of them all over, as they headed south for the winter. They migrated from Siberia and flew high over the Himalayas.

I watched as they flew on, hoping in vain that they would land in the fields.

Most of the morning was spent in that shady grove. I was lost in another man's words.

Raj's journal was written during his time in France. It was in a mixture of French and English.

But it was more than just a diary — it was a record of lives — both his and the people he'd known. I read avidly, hungrily, and was finished before noon.

My question had been answered. I now understood his solitude. I knew why he was in Dhanoa — it was his refuge — his peace with himself. And why did he seek peace? Very simply, to preserve his love for a woman.

Raj found me in the apricot grove. I had put aside his journal, and was thinking about the lives and names that I had come to know this morning, in a land so distant from here. Yet his words had filled me with sadness.

He cleared his throat softly, and sat down beside me. He had brought lunch, made by the mother of one of the children he taught.

"I finished your journal, by the way," I told him.

He said nothing and proceeded to unpack the food, which would be our main meal of the day.

He handed me a thick leavened flatbread, stuffed with onions and potatoes. And there was fresh buttermilk to wash it down with.

We ate in silence; just the rustle of the leaves kept us company.

"What took you to France?" I asked once the last drop of buttermilk had been drained. Already he had taught me not to be impatient.

Raj looked away towards the stream, where the poplars swayed.

"Oh, life, just plain, ordinary life," he said softly.

Then he added, "Did you hear the cranes a while back?"

"Yes, I did. They flew nearly over my head."

He nodded.

"They fly thousands of miles and end up here. They are at home wherever they land. In one sense, they're always returning, aren't they? Either to Russia in the summer, or the Punjab in the winter. I have always loved those cranes; I thought I was like them once."

"And now?"

"And now, I know I will not fly away again — because there's nowhere else to go to."

Yet his eyes looked up at the mountains as though he were not quite sure.

We sat without speaking, where the sunlight dappled and played, tossed from leaf to ground.

I honoured our silence for some minutes before I spoke. "I would like to copy some parts of your journal and keep them with me? I don't want to lose what I've read."

He laughed slightly.

"Is it that important?" His gaze was upon me for the first time since we'd eaten.

"May I?" I asked.

"Oh, why not," he said with an exaggerated gesture. "But what will you do with it?"

"Let's just say that it would make a fitting memento." This time, I was the one looking away. "Because it is here that I've finally found what I came to India for."

I wanted to remember this moment. I wanted to merge the fields, the poplars, the stream, the mountains, and Raj's house into one distilled memory.

"And what did you come for?" Now he was asking the hard questions.

"Peace?"

"The simplest thing to say. The hardest to find." He got to his feet. "You're welcome to copy as much of it as you want. But I have better things to do."

He gathered the lunch things and walked away. I followed after him.

Back at the house, Raj produced a small, four-stringed *tambura*-lyre and headed to his walnut tree, where he sat down on a rug woven in the village.

There, he was joined by Deva Singh, who played *tabla*-drums at the local Sikh temple. Deva came with three other young men who, it turned out, were Raj's music students.

Among other things, Raj was a singer of classical *ragas*, the melodic structures of North Indian music. This was something he had picked up from a maestro in Kashmir before he came to live in Dhanoa.

The five men beneath the walnut tree were soon lost in the timeless flow of music. That afternoon, Raj chose to sing the *raga* known as *Multani*, a characteristically Punjabi *raga*, which captures the ethos of the land of the five rivers so evocatively: dry heat, fields of wheat, flow of great rivers, and the snow-capped mountains beyond.

Each *raga* is allocated a specific time of day during which it can properly be performed, for a *raga* seeks to capture the differing moods and emotions that run through the twenty-four hours. *Multani* is an afternoon *raga*.

The words I heard Raj sing that day were in Lehndi, a northwestern dialect of Punjabi, spoken close to the Afghan border. It was like what my grandfather used to sing, casting a spell on that room in Allanville, Ontario, long ago when I was a child.

The words floated through the still, cool air:

What news does the black raven bring?
Oh my beloved, why have you gone so far away?
Is the time of your long-awaited return today?
Raven, is this news you bring?"

In the Punjab, ravens are not omens of evil and bad luck, but harbingers of joy.

That day, Raj sang for almost two hours, enraptured by the ethereal progress of the *raga*. His students added their voices, just as the birds did when Raj taught the little boys and girls in the morning.

I sat on the cot beneath the mulberry tree and began copying some of the journal entries, following the course of Raj's life in France, as if it, too, were a *raga* unfurling beneath my pen.

In my copying I do not differentiate between the French or the English; I ascribe this practice of using many languages to slippage (from one tongue to another) which polyglots, like Raj, are prone to as they search for a word, or language, that will best serve the purpose of their meaning.

"Why have you gone so far away . . . ?"

The longing in the words that Raj sang swirled around me like the limpid waters of the Piplan Nadi . . .

31

Journal Entry: Memento

How many footsteps in a lifetime? How many journeys?

Once, at least, there comes to us all the bitter gift of sorrow, with its slow rusting of the soul and ceaseless snaring of the heart that brings us to carry the burden of our bones in solitary travail, moving through the great circle of life and death, bereft of joy's rich redemption: even the reddest rose is redolent with a lover's presence or absence.

Sorrow teaches some to curse fate, to rail at God's stillness, to crave solitude and darkness. And it imparts to others the desire for unending silence of the heart that drops through the blood like a sinking stone, leaving only the briefest room for gladness, which when it comes is like the bright, brief profusion of springtime.

Sad, red rose of all our days . . .

We are all travelling towards our true home, which can be found in many forms, many sites; it is hardly ever the one we are born in.

I live in a city of rains; and as I watch this play of water, wind and earth, an incident, a conversation, a face comes to mind. It is as if these hurrying drops fall not only on greening fields, but also on the rich furrow of memory.

Today, the downpour is so thick that the drops bounce back from the cobblestones as bubbles that briefly float on the hurrying flow, bursting, disappearing in the swifter current flowing to the roadside drain.

From my window, high up on Mont-Saint-Aignan, I can see Rouen below, lying in a mantle of mist, beside the Seine. Above the mist are the high steeples of the Cathedral.

Watching this heavy rain I think back to the time when I first came to Rouen, where once stood a hundred spires, or so they say.

My train was pulling in from Paris late one January evening, and a driving rain fell like a cloak over the city and its people.

My first glimpse of Rouen from the train window was of the Cathedral, both its towers glowing with little lights that looked like opaque, barely visible stars.

At that time, I was trying to be so much, trying to do so much, and running away from so much. I wanted a place where my soul could rest and my head could clear. I knew no one in this city then; I remember I walked from the Gare all the way down rue Jeanne d'Arc to the centre of town, and found lodgings for the night in a small hotel. I had no umbrella, and I was so wet that I dripped all over the guest register, smudging many of the names of people who had stayed before me.

It wasn't too long before I got myself various odd jobs, first as kitchen help and then at a print shop, and found a little room in an old cross-timbered house on rue Boucheries.

Slowly, I settled into a quiet routine through which I learned to forget to count time's passage.

I became familiar with the shape and contours of Rouen, spending hours meandering its streets, from the bullet-riddled Palais de Justice to the statue of Napoleon in the square outside the Mairie; and I watched the Seine change from a cold grey to a muddy brown, as it carried the silent decay of civilization and nature.

Like all cities, Rouen has its own memory, filled with ancient joy and sorrow. Thomas Beckett came here when he fled from Henry's wrath; in the Cathedral William the Bastard was blessed the Conqueror; in the same church, beside the altar, the lion heart of Richard lies entombed; and in the Vieux Marché Joan of Arc was burnt into sanctity. The Romans called this city Rotomagus.

Across the street from where I lived was a little café called P'tit Parapluie. The sign showed a little red umbrella. It wasn't a particularly popular spot, with no more than a dozen customers at a time, a place where old men spent their afternoons and sometimes evenings, murmuring reminiscences to each other, giving voice to the departed world of their youth. I saw these men daily, as I came and went on the street. Each of them had a table, invisibly reserved, both inside the café and outside, at which no one else sat. The exterior stucco walls of the café were covered with a moss, whatever the season.

The patron was Monsieur Vauthier, a man in his mid-fifties, thin and tall, always in pristine suits, who entertained his guests on the piano on Friday nights. At times, a friend would accompany him on the violin. I heard them from my room, playing jazz from the '20s and '30s. His audience would listen politely, placing their orders and visiting the washroom only during the interlude between pieces. His wife was the server and the cook. Her name was Marie-Pierre, but he called her *"Mon ange."*

Friday nights still evoke a memory of that music whenever I am walking by myself, listening to my footsteps on the cobblestones: *I am in my little room again, the rain fills the night, and Monsieur Vauthier has settled into a groove, punctuated now and then by the tolling belfry of the old clock tower in the centre of town.*

One of Monsieur Vauthier's customers was a very old man who came quietly into the café, and greeted everyone with a smile before sitting down. He walked slowly with a cane and carried a slim book that was as faded as he. The table in the far corner was where he sat every day from early afternoon to evening. Monsieur Vauthier didn't mind him even though the old man never seemed to order more than a coffee or two, and only occasionally something to eat. He was one of the fixtures of the café, like the sign, the piano, the mossy walls. I looked for him whenever I passed by.

Perhaps he saw me too, as daily I hurried to somewhere or someone, caught like an autumn leaf on a swift current.

The months passed, winter slowly yielded to spring, and the dearth of March was pierced by April's ever warming rain. The air became lighter and sweeter, and the Seine cleared like well-aged cider.

With the turn of seasons, I learned a kind of contentment that comes when change is not what you desire, and the bread you eat is filled with a previously untasted sweetness.

A stillness had grown inside me that brought me the gift of fatigue at the end of day. The immediacy of merely being, filled me like a flask slowly taking in fresh, cool water from a murmuring spring deep in a Norman forest, where thickets of blackberries grow.

I would take long walks into that country, along roads that I did not know. How often I would sit beneath a tree, bring out my bread and an apple, and in the quiet of grass and dust listen to the drone of insects close by and the call of woodpigeons across the meadows. How often I would fall asleep on a mat of leaves, awaking in the dusk with the sun spilling its gold, like gilding around some miniature painting in an ancient manuscript. And I would

head back to the city, following my long shadow in the last
rays of daylight.

During the summer, Monsieur Vauthier brought some
chairs and tables outside, so that customers could look
into the courtyard of the Cathedral.

By June, there were many tourists in Rouen, but few
of them ended up at the café. Instead, they would feed
the pigeons, or peer at the Cathedral spires, the highest
in France, through their camera lenses. Others would
stand well back to take in the scenes of the two
tympanums: on the right, Christ enthroned in heaven,
and on the left, Salome standing on her hands, legs
curled forward, alluring, sensual. Herod watches her
dance, yearning for throbbing skin, promising all.
Crowded into a corner, far from this game of desire, is
John the Baptist on his knees. An executioner towers
above him, holding high a broadsword that will never fall.
In this raddled scene the Baptist is caught forever between
breath and extinction.

One afternoon as I walked past Le P'tit Parapluie, I saw
that faded old man sitting outside. He was facing the
Cathedral, watching the townsfolk and visitors busy with
their lives. On that day, for some reason, I stopped and
sat down at a nearby table.

Up close, the old gentleman was frailer than he
seemed from a distance, with hands flecked by age and
skin thin, translucent across his knuckles. He had a face
loosened by the many years he had seen, and cheeks that
were gaunt, showing veins like blue filigree. He slept, lost
to the world.

Then, there was a loud flutter of wings: a grey pigeon
with curious red eyes was staring back at me from beside

the old man's coffee cup. It swayed its head indecisively from side to side.

The old man was awake now, but sat unmoving. He looked at me in a conspiratorial way, as if to say, "Be still. Don't frighten it."

After cooing quickly and looking at the table to make sure there were no crumbs about, the pigeon leaped up and took wing again; it circled the narrow sliver of sky between the Cathedral walls and then slowly floated away towards the roofs of the cross-timbered houses.

The old man laughed quietly, then looked at me, inviting me to share in his mirth.

"Do you read poetry, young man?"

I was taken aback. "Well, yes," I said, "as a matter of fact I do."

He held out the blue-covered book I'd seen him carry.

"Take a look and tell me what you think," he said, his voice trailing off, as though embarrassed by his forwardness.

I opened the book and read the title page: *Le nuage et la voile, une rêverie en vers, par M Henri Méliton. Éditions Apollon. Reims, 1913.*

The pages were brittle at the edges, and yellowed with age.

"Are you Monsieur Méliton?"

"Oh no, no. I am not a poet; just someone who likes to read poetry now and then. It's all so long ago, now."

I read a brief quatrain that was entitled *"La chasse"* ('The Hunt'): *Dans le silence le patelin dorme . . .*

In the silence the village sleeps at night,
but the hunter's eye has forgotten sleep . . .

I closed the book and held it out to give back. But he seemed not to notice; and after an awkward moment, I put it beside my cup. He had closed his eyes and was sleeping again.

I ordered another coffee and re-opened the book. This time the poem before me was called *"La langueur"* ('Languor'):

How softly floats the boatman's slow evening song
Like an odalisque holding a folded fan . . .

I turned the page and read another piece called *"Le grimpereau"* ('The Creeper'):

What parched desire
Climbs out of these trees
And does not tire?

They were amusing, slight little poems, quickly forgotten, shards of times long lost, brief glimmers from the *Belle Époque.*

I wondered what happened to Monsieur Méliton the poet.

The old man stirred, his eyes were open.

"He was a good man. Quiet. Said very little. He looked so awkward in his captain's uniform. We were all so young then. He was killed on the Meuse in 1914, shot through the stomach. We found him sitting on his haunches in our trench, as if he were about to leap up."

He had answered my unspoken question. I looked across at him. His faded eyes were seeing a different world. I, the café, this city did not exist.

"His personal effects were given to me since I knew him. Among them I found photos of him and a young woman, smiling, happy. I have them still at home; there they lie, yellowing, unknown. But that is death, is it not? There was also a woman's ring. I don't know whose it was. I shall never know." His voice was no longer frail, but surprisingly clear and deep.

He closed his eyes again; but this time he didn't go to sleep. Perhaps he wanted to clear away the vanished world of his youth, so he could return to this one, where I sat holding the words of a man long dead.

"Did you see inside the cover?"

I hadn't. I opened the book again and found a dedication:

Marguerite,
qu'une année de joies commence pour toi cette nuit,
petite amie, et que toute peine te soit épargnée.
31 Déc. 1913
Eugène Fasquelle.

(Marguerite, May a year of joys begin for you this night, sweetheart, and may pain never touch you. 31st of December, 1913. Eugène Fasquelle).

The old man spoke on, with his eyes closed, his voice strong, his words fluent.

"Quite a while back, I was staying in Paris with my son, who is also an old man now; and during one of my morning walks across the Pont des Arts I came across someone selling old books, all neatly laid out on a large table. It was a very clear morning, bright and cool. Out of habit, I began to sift through what he had, and I selected one. The vendor wanted fifty francs for it; I gave him what he asked. I must say he was surprised that I didn't haggle. And I took that book and have carried it with me ever since."

The bells in the clock tower slowly chimed.

"I am now ninety-six-years-old. I am frail but still healthy. I've had a good life. I've been happy and sad. Do you think time makes old wounds less painful? I used to think so, until that clear bright morning in Paris. Now, all my sorrow is fresh before me."

He had retreated back into his world beyond most living memories.

I looked at the book again; gently placed it near his right hand.

He quietly picked it up and smiled sadly, distantly, as though greeting all those he once knew. Then he sighed, looked at his bill, put down two ten-franc coins, tore up the bill and slowly got up.

As he gathered himself, he turned again to me and said, "You see, I am Eugène Fasquelle; the one who wrote that ardent inscription. I don't know what happened to Marguerite after the war. I looked everywhere, but she was gone."

And he slowly walked away, the cane in his right hand, the book in his left . . .

There were more pigeons on the cobblestones, pecking away at seeds and crumbs unseen, encouraged by the presence of more tourists.

I never saw that old man again.

Sometime in late August, Monsieur Vauthier suddenly died. His wife, who was not from Rouen but from a small village in Picardy, sold the P'tit Parapluie to someone who converted it within weeks into an art supply store.

And one day, as I watched from my window, two burly, red-faced men panted and grunted and heaved the piano into a decrepit truck; shouted loudly and drove off in a cloud of acrid, black smoke.

As the truck pulled away, the clock in the belfry tolled ten times that bright morning. The sign with the little red umbrella was painted over with plain black lettering: *Gallerie de tableaux.*

The store attracted a lot of people.

Soon after, I moved from that little room on rue Boucheries, and even now do not go into that part of the city . . .

CHAPTER 4

LIKE THE VILLAGERS OF DHANOA, I fell into a daily routine: up by eight, a quick bath, breakfast, work on the journal, lunch, a few hours of wandering about, back to the village, dinner, conversation with Raj, and bed by ten o'clock.

I would watch the village boys take the cattle to the Piplan Nadi for the weekly scrub down of the animals.

Those patient beasts sank up to their ears, while all around them the boys yelled and screeched as they splashed about in the frigid waters of the smooth-backed stream. I, too, experienced this iciness every morning and evening, in bucketfuls, during my baths.

Each day waxed, grew old, died, as the night above us spread wide her robe of stars. The lowing of cattle in their folds was as old as the land.

"I chose this village to live in because I thought here I would taste life in its simplicity," Raj told me one evening. Far ahead of us the snowy tops of the Himalayas gleamed in the blanched moonlight.

"But I was chasing a chimera that would serve to remind me of what I once had, all of which you have read about in my journal. There is no fiction in what you read. Between those covers is my life in France." Raj's voice softened.

"There is no such thing as a simple life. Even here in Dhanoa, there is complexity and confusion and hurt." He put back his head: *"The body that does not grieve, yearn, or sorrow . . . "*

He was quoting from the words of the *raga* that he'd sang earlier that afternoon; a couplet in fact from Baba Farid, the twelfth-century Punjabi Sufi saint:

We all cry out in grief, yearning, sorrow:
these rule the world.
The body that does not grieve, yearn, or sorrow
is barren as a cremation field . . .

The next morning, as I walked back from the stream, I saw a *saadh*, or a holy man, sitting beneath the walnut tree; he must have come during the night; I hadn't noticed him as I went to wash up.

I walked over. Before I could greet him, I recognized him. It was the old man who had helped me on the day of the car crash. That seemed so long ago, now, and I could scarcely believe that I had not recognized him as a saddh.

"Pa khair? All is well?" He asked me in Pashto. "So, you're still here." He motioned me to sit beside him.

"But where did you go?" I asked. "I didn't see you after the day you rescued me."

"Oh, I move around a lot." There was that mischievous smile again. "This is a big country, you know."

I asked him to join us for a cup of tea and breakfast. He accepted cheerfully, and followed me to Raj's house.

When we entered, Raj greeted the old man warmly, and the two of them sat on the cot beneath the mulberry tree.

"I'll get some bread," I said, as I headed out the door again.

There was a crowd already at the communal oven, eager to get the leavened flatbread. I bought some, along with butter and headed back.

Tea was waiting, upon my return, and the three of us broke bread together.

The old man's name was Bawa Dayal, and he really was a *saadh*, or a holy man; he belonged to the *Udasi* sect, whose members wander the earth either as mendicants, or follow the more settled ways of married temple priests, exegetes of scripture, or performers of religious duties and rituals.

Raj addressed him as "Bawa-ji," a term of respect meaning "revered abbot." I followed suit.

Bawa-ji followed the path of charity and charted the deep contours of his soul — but he did it with a joyous glimmer in his eye and a hearty laugh.

It was the first week of October, and the days were very cool.

After breakfast, Raj headed off to teach. This morning, the children would use the apricot grove as their classroom, since Bawa-ji now sat beneath the walnut tree absorbed in meditation.

I accompanied Raj to fetch some water to wash dishes with.

"Do you speak French well?" Raj asked me.

"I do a little, as I told you." I replied.

"Do you mind if I practice my French with you. It's been a long time since I've spoken it with anyone. Since the day I handed you my journal, I've been thinking about France. I suddenly feel like an outsider again, and I wish the days of happiness would come back — even just once."

"No, I don't mind at all." I slowly lowered a bucket into the rushing stream and watched it fill. "But I fear *il faut que vous parlera bien lentement,* and you may find my accent as strange as my Punjabi."

He laughed. "We'll manage, I'm sure. Thank you for humouring me."

He walked quickly over the unsteady rope bridge and I lost sight of him as he entered the grove.

It was with that peculiar request that Raj began to unfurl before me his wisdom and his sorrow.

From that day onwards, he and I conversed regularly in French. There, in Dhanoa, just north of Manali, we would sit and remember the words of Rimbaud, or speak of the tragic life of Charles d'Orleans whose poetry is a memory of his homeland when he sat in an English prison for more than twenty years; and once, via a cassette tape by Paul Tortelier, even Louis XIV's great violist, Marin Marais, found his way to Dhanoa, where in a little wattle-and-daub house, he revealed his sonorous, deep caprices, folies, suites and *tombeaux . . .*

This mixture of France and the Punjab was not so exotic as it might seem, because in the court of Maharajah Ranjit Singh, the great king whom some call the "Lion of the Punjab", there were many French officers who trained the Sikh armies. They were mercenaries who had come to India after the defeat of Napoleon at Waterloo, and had set themselves up as military advisors to the Maharajah, carrying on their fight against the English on different soil.

They were all flamboyant characters: General Allard, who married a pretty young Kashmiri girl, and in his old age went back to Paris; there was General Court who insisted on drilling the troops no matter what the weather; the good Dr. Benet who was appointed the chief court physician.

45

And then there was the traveller Victor Jacquemont, who tells us that during royal feasts the courtiers threw gold dust on each other, so by the end of the evening everyone glowed like gods in the torchlight; he also mentions the Maharajah's penchant for strong drink, especially a distillation of pure spirit derived from macerated lion's meat in which were dissolved black pearls.

Many at the court spoke fluent French, and other languages too, since there were Irish, Italian, German, Spanish, Scottish, Russian, and American mercenaries as well.

And long before them, there were the travellers from the court of Louis XIV.

Jean-Baptiste Tavernier, who so meticulously categorized diamonds by their water, clarity and weight and single-handedly created a market for gemstones in Europe. And one day, in 1642, he bought a diamond of the first water, deep blue, rare, large as a hen's egg, which he sold to his king for a modest sum. Today it is known as the Hope Diamond, the bauble of film stars, insured for millions.

Tavernier was followed by the physician François Bernier, in 1652, who made his way right up to Kashmir, meticulously recording what he saw.

So when Raj and I spoke French, it was not entirely without precedent.

And who knows, at Versailles, a *saadh* might have been found, sitting beneath a towering pine, in the early afternoon, solemnly chanting the ancient *Gayatri mantra*, which is a prayer, an offering, a blessing: "May Savitr, the sun, shine on us all; may we become golden as the gods . . ."

Journal Entry: Mathilde

In the hush of mist-laden Sunday mornings, there are two sounds that mark the start of day: the sonorous bells of distant churches, and the shrieks of quarrelling magpies that come visiting my backyard. They're louder than dogs, as they swagger about, their long black tails dipping with each step, their white-patched wings spread to thwart any darting sparrows. But theirs is a brief reign that ends with a cat's snarl. And off they go to brawl in another yard.

When I first moved up to Mont-Saint-Aignan from downtown Rouen, now all those years ago, I got up early with the church bells and the magpies to watch the mist slowly melt in the sun, or be washed away by the rain, like the lumps of sugar dissolving in my bright blue coffee bowl.

But constancy still eluded my grasp like a fading echo.

Mont-Saint-Aignan is a peculiar place, perched high atop one of the hills that surround Rouen. It doesn't have much to offer: most of the buildings are shabby, deteriorating cement boxes, the university being the prime example of this type of architecture. But I am reminded by friends that during the last war, most of this area was bombed relentlessly, and it was a tough fight to get rid of the Nazi *Chleuh*.

On Sunday afternoons I would go for walks, following the road beside my house all the way down to the Hôtel Bellevuc 'til I reached the Abbey of St. Jacques — now only a few Romanesque arches, bordered on the east side by a passementerie of grotesque, carved faces.

There isn't much to see. Inside the arches a narrow stone sarcophagus lies empty in a corner. I've seen young boys play tennis against the inside walls, which have been extensively restored. The building is a beautiful fragment that lies on a rising green knoll, where a fresh breeze is always to be found in the summer. Are not all fragments beautiful because they are so brief? We were never meant to hold them in their fullness, for their essence has vanished like the hands that once brought them into being.

On the south wall, a plaque informs the visitor that in this Abbey, Thomas Beckett sought refuge when he ran from England, flying before the fury of his king and friend. Just above are two fantastical, salamander-like creatures, clinging, frozen in stone.

The locals pay little attention to this trace of antiquity. They ignore it, or stop to let their dogs urinate against the arches; there are even the ubiquitous spray-painted gang signatures of late on the east wall. I've never seen any one really visit this place — not even tourists.

It was first shown to me by Mathilde just before I moved up to Mont-Saint-Aignan; Mathilde whose eyes were as green as the deepest forests of her land.

I would sit on the knoll staring at the ancient stone, hewn by nameless hands, with the timeless sky above me; I would be joined by the magpies that milled around, unafraid, squawking, their eyes greedy, their beaks open for a quarrel. But then I did bring them my day-old stub of a baguette.

One among them stood out. While the rest were quick and loud, he was slow and had badly frayed tail-feathers. He reminded me of an old, toothless sailor who has been in one bar brawl too many. He had even lost the shrill notes of his cry. When he opened his mouth, only a loud rasp came out. He never shied away from me and was happy to eat out of my hand; this way he did not have to fight with the others for every crumb.

Whenever I came to the Abbey, he was there, waiting for the stale baguette that the night had turned hard as stone, which I crumbled for him.

I'm sure he waited for me every afternoon, whether or not I could keep the tryst.

I named him *Pipeau le pie.*

After feeding Pipeau and some of his friends, I would go down to Rouen and visit Mathilde.

She lived in a small flat just behind rue Fontenelle, above a pastry shop. Her rooms smelled of baking and old wood.

Mathilde studied music and had curious instruments from around the world. Her favourite was an alto recorder made of ebony, with an ivory mouthpiece. She played it occasionally and very carefully. It could not be forced, she said. There was a resonance in that instrument which gave vibrancy to the simple airs that Mathilde played on it.

When her breath gave tone to the recorder, it was as if all the musicians, who in the past had given it breath, came flocking to that little room, pulled by the memory of life's sweetness. Each note brought them briefly again into the brightness of the sun — all those long departed into the depths of the earth.

When I held her, Mathilde's body softened in my arms, and her mouth tasted of ancient wood.

Her family had a medieval farm near where the River Eure meets the Seine, and where both rivers slow to wind and curve around little villages and steep bluffs. Not far from their place was Château Gaillard, the steep castle built on a mountain crag by Richard the Lionhearted.

Her mother, Madame Hardouin, was never short of fresh bread, hot from the oven, the conical chimney of which sent up wisps of blue smoke that could be seen from afar. Her father made his own calvados, whose every sip reminded me of apple orchards, and his own camembert, which lay in white, crusted rounds wrapped in straw.

Mathilde and I went on long picnics in the country, taking with us the hamper her mother would pack. Inside, we would find bread, cheese, a bottle of homemade cider, foie gras, tartelets, a salad of some sort, and a bottle each of water and red wine.

We would get in the car, her blue Citroen, and drive out into the Seine Valley and wander about in the forest of Vernon, with the high cliffs beyond. We would talk of many things and finally eat beneath the branches of an ancient beech. She taught me how to seek out the rare *mourie* mushrooms that are hardly found in markets, because villagers warily safeguard the places where they grow.

We could never finish all that was in the hamper. But as Madame Hardouin said, it was good to have more than less, and it was good to bring some back than to run out.

Once we drove around for two weeks from Amiens to Bayeux, from Chartres to Anger, staying at little *auberges*, never in a hurry. And it was in Anger, one evening, I remember, on an old Roman bridge, by the green waters of the Loire, that Mathilde suddenly hugged me and began to cry. She never told me why her tears fell on my shoulder. And now it's too late to ask.

The days we spent together rushed from one to another like a flashing stream in a glade. I remember how happy I was watching Mathilde steering her Citroen, laughing, continuously talking, falling silent only when I reached out to touch her hair, or her hand.

We would go to the beach at Dieppe, the closest one for the inhabitants of Rouen; its shoreline has no sand but consists of large, smooth pebbles that pockmark the bodies of sunbathers. It is very hard to walk on this shifting bed.

And it was here that the expeditionary raiders ran for cover, in August of 1942, strafed by machine gun fire. The Germans were ready, waiting.

Beyond the cliffs, in the commune of Hautôt-sur-Mer, over nine hundred lie in long double rows, Americans, Britons, Canadians, buried head-to-head.

Whenever we went there, that long gone August day played out its ferocity around me: the clinging smell of cordite, oily smoke, the clatter of pebbles falling back after an explosion, screams, confusion, the strong odour of burnt flesh . . .

But all that has been washed from the shore by the waters of the English Channel, where the River Arques empties, and where bare-breasted women bathe in the warm summer sun.

Like all harbour towns, Dieppe is a place filled with people who look rough and forgotten, and who perhaps should have moved on a long time ago, but didn't. The town was once famous for its ivory-works, but none of that grandeur remains. The thirteenth-century church of St. Jacques that squats in the centre of town is the most dilapidated place of worship that I have ever seen in France.

The Normans were Viking settlers, and "Dieppe" is a Norse word meaning "deep water." My first image of this city is of two stray cats fighting over freshly severed fishheads and viscera by the docks.

Whenever we returned from Dieppe, usually in the evening, we showered, changed, and went to an outdoor café to sip some wine, and talk of the day we'd spent together.

For how many Sundays I fed Pipeau that summer, I cannot now remember. And as summer, too, grew old, there were less companions with him; they had probably found a richer food supply over my meager crumbs. This likely suited Pipeau very well, since competition was less.

At that time, I had a job translating very thick, closely written business manuals, from French into English; the routine was numbing. So it was a joy when, in late September, Mathilde asked me if I would help her father press apples for a week; she would stay at the farm, too.

Work began early at the Hardouin farm; and when dawn broke above the rows of nearly naked apple trees, we had cleaned the millstones, scrubbing them with wet straw, then rinsing them with water.

All around us were mounds of apples, each one a different variety. Monsieur Hardouin pointed them out to me, as we scrubbed.

Every day we would press two kinds; and in order not to adulterate the taste, everything would be hosed down before starting the second batch.

On the first day, we pressed the Charge-Souvent and A la Faux apples. On the following day, we did the Carnette and De la Banque apples. Then came the Mettais, Tête de Brebis, the De Cheminée and the Gros Moussette. And on the last day, we pressed the Medaille d'Or apples, for good luck — as Monsieur Hardouin remarked, *"Cela porte bonheur!"*

After we had carted the apples to the press, which needed two men to turn, we watched the fruit being changed into a steady flow of golden juice that ran along a wooden trough into a large oak barrel. After an initial pressing, the millstones were loosened and a fresh layer of straw was added; then the press was tightened and turned again to extract the last drop of juice. The rusting pulp we gave over to the pigs.

The work was done with frequent recourse to song interspersed with comments on how clear the juice trickled this year, and how strong the cider would be. The air held the fragrance of apples and damp straw, as if spring were again awakening the orchard outside.

At the end of the week, Monsieur Hardouin had more than twenty barrels of juice.

In a few days he would begin the fermentation; and before winter he would draw a clear spout of straw-coloured, strong cider that never failed to remind one of blossoming orchards, no matter how deep the snow outside.

More than half this cider would be further refined into calvados, that fierce brandy which retains the fragrance of burgeoning Norman apple groves like a delicious memory.

Thus passed my first summer and autumn in Mont-Saint-Aignan; it had surprisingly not rained that much.

In mid-October, Mathilde told me that she was going to Strasbourg to further her musical career. She wanted to sing and record little ballads: her soul "was a hart that sought high waters," and her voice "would never know silence." She wanted to learn to play different instruments, see different cultures, learn different languages; but most of all she wanted to sing.

By late October, the rains came, and Mathilde was ready to move. She went home first for a week, and then returned to Rouen; she spent the last day with me.

Deep in the night, I awoke and looked at her sleeping body; her dark hair draped the side of her face, and her long-fingered hand rested on the high, tube pillow; her face was like a pond, clear and deep, and her breasts rose and fell with her breathing. I watched her in sadness: how fleeting everything can be when a heart cannot be held. I greedily sought her warmth for the last time.

Next morning, her luggage and instrument cases lay neatly packed by the door, while my own things cluttered the room. We had breakfast and went to the Gare, where her train waited.

There was nothing to say; instead we checked and re-checked her train ticket, her money, and her ID card.

"The express for Strasbourg will leave in five minutes from Platform 2." The metallic voice announced over the station intercom.

We hurried over to Platform 2, and Mathilde boarded, and I carried in her baggage. We hugged and said goodbye; there were no tears. Before I got down from the train, she formally kissed me on both cheeks.

Through the window her green eyes looked down at me; she gave me a quick little smile, folded her arms and leaned against the pane. As the train pulled away, she briefly waved, and was gone.

Afterwards, I went back up to Mont-Saint-Aignan, stopping at the *boulangerie* where Mathilde had lived.

Pipeau was waiting for me, even though it wasn't Sunday.

I broke off some bread, and he ate it greedily. But he didn't stay long.

With a rasp that seemed less loud, he flew up and perched on the grinning face of a Wodwo.

Then he leapt up again, and began to float clumsily down from the mountain to the busy city below.

As I watched him fly away, I knew he would not survive the winter.

Mathilde answered some of my letters, but she was moving further and further away — first to Italy, then to Turkey, and on to India.

The last time I heard from her she was in Australia, and she sent me a tape of her songs that she had made there. It was a special surprise for me, she said.

The first song began with her playing her alto recorder; I could see her beautiful fingers moving to fashion the slow melody. And these were the words she sang: *"Flee far off into the future, far from mankind, until time too is old. Thus I speak to sorrow that cannot know the flowing heart . . . "*

Journal Entry: The King

Tucked away in one of the sterile cement blocks, high up in Mont-Saint-Aignan, lived Charlot, a heavy-set man in his early seventies. His white hair fanned around his head like an aura, and his tiny dark eyes darted around as if searching for something he'd lost a long time ago.

I got to know Charlot at the Bar Safari, an incongruous drinking hole with ancient posters of African wildlife and a few dusty, stuffed animals, which supposedly had been bagged by Monsieur Poussin, the owner of the Bar, on his one and only expedition to Africa. He was a thin, agile man, who moved about with lightning speed, with always an apt remark on his lips. He was in his mid-forties.

Monsieur Poussin regaled all and sundry with hunting stories that changed and grew with every drink you ordered; the more you drank the more stories came gushing out of Monsieur Poussin's endless word-hoard. And if you showed little enthusiasm about tales of bringing down large beasts with a single, well-placed shot, then Monsieur Poussin would be more than happy to switch subjects, in mid-flight, and tell you all about the sexual prowess of African women. With a glint in his eye, he would insist that the Berber woman did something special with her hips, while the Massai woman was graceful yet had great staying power.

These stories never ceased, and in the years I knew Monsieur Poussin, I was amazed at the length and breadth of his experiences in Africa. Of course, it wasn't long before someone told me that the furthest Monsieur Poussin had gotten on African soil was Rabat in Morocco, when he went on a guided tour with his old mother, who had passed away a few years earlier.

The Bar Safari had a regular clientele, men who lived in the neighbourhood, mostly in the grey low-rises that had been built in the 1960s but now looked like the worst excesses of Stalin's socialist-realist architecture; in short, ugly as Hell; the kind that can suck the soul out of a human being in a single day. And yet people lived happily there, I'm sure, and I felt a twinge of guilt in that I judged harshly. Certainly, my own habitation was nothing to brag about: it was a cement low-rise too, but built in the 1980s, so it had a fresher wash of stucco.

The bar stayed open until 4:00 A.M., but the clientele never changed much, except that after midnight weary-looking prostitutes wondered in frequently for a quick coffee before heading back out into the fray.

It was past midnight on a rainy October night, and I sat with my drink, listening to the noise around me, with Monsieur Poussin's voice, as always, the loudest. This time, he had something to say about the prostitutes of Rabat, the size of their breasts, and what could be done with them. He told the story to no one in particular; rather to anyone who cared to listen.

I was sitting at a table, since there was no room yet at the bar proper. Not far from me sat an old man, huddled into his chair, as if trying to ward off the damp and the cold. He clutched his shot of brandy desperately in a huge, pudgy hand. In the dim light, his hair seemed to glow, pale and phosphorescent. This was Charlot.

His face was vacant, unknowable. Whether from too much drink, or too much loneliness, I could not at that time have guessed.

He drained his shot, and unsteadily rose to get another. Monsieur Poussin had no wait staff, and if you wanted a drink, you had to get it yourself and pay immediately.

When he returned to his seat, he sat staring at me. I raised my glass and drank.

Charlot, too, raised his glass in an unsteady toast, and tossed back his drink.

Then he rose again and returned with a beer. He sat down, but no longer looked at me.

Raising his fist high above him, Charlot brought it down with a resounding thump. No one bothered to turn around. I looked at him, thinking any minute now Monsieur Poussin would scurry out from behind the bar and shove Charlot out the door.

"My king! My king! They hanged my king! In front of my very own eyes!" Shouted Charlot at the top of his voice, as his fist pounded the table.

"Hey, Charlot, shut up, or out you go!" Monsieur Poussin bellowed.

Charlot immediately sank back into his silence, nursing his beer and his soul.

I could hear him whimper now then, repeating the same phrase over and over again.

"My king. Why did they hang you? My king. My king. My king."

His whimper soon became a barely audible wail.

I went and sat beside him; he didn't notice I was there.

"Don't worry about poor Charlot. Once he gets like that it's best to leave him alone," Monsieur Poussin blared at me.

Reluctantly, I went and sat at the bar, where there was now some room, and ordered another drink.

A trio of prostitutes scampered in, ordered coffees, downed them in a flash and went out the door, leaving a lingering trace of perfume, not at all unpleasant.

In one of the rare lulls in Monsieur Poussin's stream of narrative, I asked about Charlot, and what he meant by his "king."

Monsieur Poussin looked furtively at Charlot, twirled his forefinger near the side of his head and let out a long, low whistle.

"He looks more drunk than crazy to me," I responded.

"He's worse when he's sober," Monsieur Poussin grunted.

I asked again about his "king."

"That, my friend, is a long story," said Monsieur Poussin, though without his usual enthusiasm.

"Will you tell it to me?"

And tell me he did, while the others at the bar listened in silence.

This was no breast-fondling, rhino-chasing extravaganza; it was almost the saddest story I've ever heard.

Charlot was a war orphan, and during those Nazi years, he was a professional street urchin, a master of his trade. Near and far he was renowned for his ability to pick any kind of pocket, no matter how well concealed. His was a natural talent, Monsieur Poussin confided.

During those years, Charlot had a companion, an older boy; the two were inseparable. They looked after each other and split whatever they earned in a day.

This was also the time of the French Underground, the Maquis, who were busy with their own war against the hated *Chleuhs*.

Down the mountain in Rouen, right by the Donjon, where Joan of Arc had been held, was the Gestapo headquarters. And some people in the Underground — just local townsmen, Monsieur Poussin explained — decided one day that enough was enough and they were going to show the *Chleuhs* a thing or two. So they began making this elaborate plan to kill some Germans. Now in those days, it was enough just to want to kill Germans; you didn't need a plan more elaborate than that.

Here, Monsieur Poussin paused and leaned heavily against the bar; he was suddenly, uncharacteristically, distant, perhaps even pensive.

Someone pushed an empty glass across the bar, and he filled it in silence, before he continued the story.

And so the day came when three self-styled Maquisards got themselves ready and checked and rechecked their pistols. They weren't killers. No man among them had even slaughtered a chicken.

But off they went, just before sunrise, down to Rouen, to wait for some *Chleuh* officer to drive by.

Now there was one particular German soldier at the time, who lived close to the Donjon. He wasn't Gestapo or even an officer; just an ordinary soldier. He had fallen in love with this girl from Canteleu named Florence, and he lived with her in an apartment. His name was Sigmund; a nice young man of maybe twenty, conscripted like so many others against his will. He hated the war, but he was happy in Rouen, with his Florence from Canteleu. They were in love, and were hated for it by some citizens. But they cared little what other people thought. Monsieur Poussin shrugged. They were happy and that was that.

Now Sigmund was on night patrol that month, and he came home to Florence just before sunrise. She would be waiting for him with hot coffee and some bread and butter, for certainly those with German connections ate better than most people.

Now our three commandos had been standing around waiting for a German officer to show up for quite some time. They were all tired and frustrated, their drinks were wearing off, and most of them wanted to go home, or at least have an early morning beer. There wasn't a German in sight until Sigmund came whistling along on his bicycle, his rifle slung carelessly across his back.

Still whistling, he hopped off his bike, and opened the gate to go inside the courtyard of the building where he and Florence lived.

He whistled softly, but Florence could hear it a mile off, she swore, and the minute she heard it, she poured out his coffee and put in the three lumps of sugar he liked.

"He's a *Chleuh*, isn't he?" One of the would-be assassins whispered.

"It's only Sigmund. He's harmless, and he's not even an officer."

"Doesn't matter. He's a *Chleuh!*"

Sigmund saw the three men running towards him; he knew them. One of them he had even bought drinks for, from time to time.

But now he was just a *Chleuh* — Monsieur Poussin shrugged again — and that was that.

Perhaps Sigmund was going to ask what they were running for, but he never got the chance.

The three of them ran up close, leveled their pistols and blazed away. They were gone before he hit the ground, and the noise of the shots brought Florence racing down. With a piercing shriek she fell on her knees beside Sigmund, holding his limp head in her hands.

Monsieur Poussin stared past me, as if he were watching the scene. It was too late, he sighed. Sigmund had slipped away beyond all knowing. And Florence? She wailed like an animal for a very long time, he said. Most people who saw her, turned away, muttering that the whore deserved it for sleeping with a *Chleuh*.

But that wasn't the end of it. Sigmund, after all, was a German soldier, and France was under German rule. The Germans weren't going to let this outrage pass unanswered. The matter was put in the hands of the Gestapo just down the street.

There were murmurs along the bar. Fresh drinks were poured. Clearly they'd all heard the story before, but it held them spellbound. And so it did me, as I listened to what happened next.

The Gestapo went all over Rouen, with loudspeakers demanding that the assassins be handed over, within three hours.

The three hours came and went, and nothing happened. Then they announced that everybody was to gather at the Cathedral Square.

People went mostly out of curiosity.

German soldiers were lined up everywhere, and one of their trucks sat right in front of the Cathedral, with its tarp removed. Four men were inside.

A Gestapo officer announced that everyone was to watch in silence. No one could look away. Those who did would be shot.

Then they brought a youth, no more than seventeen. He was stripped to the waist, his eyes swollen with too many tears. He was struggling and begging, but the men holding him were indifferent to his pleas.

The Gestapo officer nodded and stepped back.

Two soldiers dangled the boy from the truck, while a third soldier quickly put a loop of piano wire around his neck.

Then they let the boy drop. He dangled there from the truck, his feet just inches from the ground. He thrashed about, desperately clawing at the thin wire that was slowly slicing into his neck. The Gestapo hadn't even tied his hands, knowing full well there was no way he could free himself.

Not a sound came from the gathered crowd. There was just heard the thrashing of the boy's feet against the truck's body, beating sporadically like the dying heart in his breast. His pants were soaked through with his own piss.

They let him dangle until his neck was nearly sliced through, and when it was, his feet came to rest limply on the ground.

The crowd was completely still; you couldn't hear a single breath, or a cough, or even the shuffle of feet.

And then came a long howl from a single throat.

"Nooo!"

Then some more words:

"My king! My king! My king!"

It was Charlot, howling with grief.

You see, this boy the Germans killed as an example was known by the street urchins as "The King," since he looked after them all.

He was also the constant companion of the young Charlot. They were like brothers.

When the King was dead, the Germans cut the wire, and let his body fall to the spattered cobblestones.

Then the Gestapo officer stepped forward. They would keep killing one youth or child everyday, he announced, until the assassins were handed over.

Well, you can be sure the next day they had the three men who shot Sigmund. The Gestapo executed them, of course, dumped their bodies in the Seine. No was allowed to fish them out.

"Ever since that day, poor Charlot has never been the same. He has never forgotten his King."

Monsieur Poussin turned and reached for a bottle from the shelf. He poured himself a drink, and then one for me.

"You're wondering how come I know all this." He sighed heavily; placed his drink on the bar; looked at it reflectively, then lifted up the glass and drained it.

He looked at me with a sad little smile.

"I know, my friend, because Florence was my mother, and, *evidemment*, that Sigmund was my father. And my mother took care of Charlot. In one sense, he is my older brother."

I turned to look at Charlot, still clutching his drink, eyes closed, still whimpering: "My king . . . My king . . . "

Outside the Bar Safari, dawn was just beginning to tug another day into all of our lives.

CHAPTER 5

AS A CHILD, RAJ GREW UP IN ENGLAND, near the Scottish border, where so many Punjabis had settled. He had gone there with his parents when he was about ten-years-old. His father was a teacher of mathematics.

Yet it was France, he told me, that he visited in his dreams.

Upon waking, though, he would find himself on his little cot, in Dhanoa — and everything at that moment would be foreign to him. He would call out in French or English. No one would reply. He would be alone, homeless, without friends or family, lost in some unknown land. His heart would race. He would call again. And the sounds of Dhanoa would come to him: the cowbells, the stray dogs, the nightingales — from which, in that dark hour, he derived no comfort. But where could he run? Where could he go? A broken heart is like a scarred face: it perpetually seeks to hide.

He was the eldest of three children. When he was eighteen, his parents and his brother and sister died together. All he would say was that there had been a boating accident.

After months of aimless wandering, he accepted the invitation of some of his father's friends and went South and enrolled at Goldsmith College in London. But instead of completing his studies, he chose to roam, travelling through the continent, living for a few months in Germany, Italy, Greece, Spain, Belgium, Holland. It was France, however, that held him. He stayed on, finding a life for himself in Rouen.

One day, while Raj was busy with his teaching and Bawa-ji was deep in his meditation, I wandered through the village and found myself in the local Sikh temple, where the *mahant*, Pundit Prem, was conducting the afternoon service, singing verses from the *Granth Sahib*, the Sikh holy book. The musicians accompanying him were Deva Singh on the *tabla*-drums, and Gurmukh, the *mahant*'s son, on the *rabaab*, which is like a fiddle.

The *mahant*, like Bawa-ji, was also an *Udasi*, the sect started by Sri Chand, the son of Guru Nanak, the founder of the Sikh religion.

Sri Chand accepted his father's reformation of Hinduism by way of Sufism, but chose to follow the mendicant path as the one truly suited for him. He said that just as his father had reformed Hinduism, he would reform the *saadh* tradition, by advocating social responsibility as an integral part of meditation. The result was the *Udasi* sect, whose members could either have families, or live as recluses.

I noticed that the *mahant* was also a *sehajdhaari* Sikh, or those who did not join the militarized sect within Sikhism, the Khalsas, created by the tenth Sikh guru, Gobind Singh in 1699, to fight Muslim oppression.

Guru Gobind Singh initiated external symbols of active Khalsa Sikhism, chief among them the wearing of the hair and beard unshorn for one's entire life.

The *sehajdhaaris* were those Sikhs who told Guru Gobind Singh that they would abstain from his militant sect and continue following the earlier pacifist, mystical traditions preached by the previous gurus; *sehajdhaari* means "slow conformers." However, the *sehajdhaaris* did support the Guru's struggles against Muslim persecution.

And it was in the time of these struggles that the control of temples was handed over to *mahants*, who did not have long hair or beards, and therefore could not be easily identified as Sikhs. This allowed Sikh temples to continue as living institutions, which could also be used as bases for resistance. It was also during this time that a bounty was placed on Sikhs — one severed Sikh head could be traded for a pound of silver.

As I entered the temple, I covered my head with a handkerchief, bowed in obeisance to the holy book, made an offering of money, took *parshaad* (a sweet *halva* of flour fried in butter, a communion of sorts) and sat down on the carpeted floor to the right, for women sit separately to the left.

The holy words purled around me. I had never been to a Sikh temple before. I sensed a peace encroaching to fill my heart: was this the Punjab I searched for — spiritual, vigorously rustic, poetic, pragmatic, militaristic and pacifist, a land where contradictions harmonized . . . ?

Rama died, and even Ravana died,
who had a huge family.
Nanak says, Nothing is eternal:
the world is like a dream.

Thus sang the Pundit. They were the words of Tegh Bahadur, the ninth Sikh Guru, and were written while the Guru was imprisoned in Delhi by the Mughal Emperor Aurangzeb.

The Guru had asked the Emperor to relent on his ruthless and constant campaigns of converting Hindus to Islam.

The Brahmins of Kashmir, whom Aurangzeb was forcibly seeking to convert, had implored Guru Tegh Bahadur to intervene on their behalf. The Guru travelled to Delhi to lodge a protest and was promptly arrested, thrown into prison, and given the same choice as the Kashmiri Brahmins: convert or die.

The Guru tried to reason with Aurangzeb, saying that all paths to God were true, and that God was the end of all religions. But the Emperor was inflexible and ordered the Guru be executed by public beheading.

Awaiting death, Guru Tegh Bahadur wrote a series of quatrains, filled with the wisdom, courage, and faith of a man living out his last days.

On the day of his execution, Guru Tegh Bahadur said to the Emperor that he had given his head, but not his essence.

Afterwards, faithful followers, in the dead of night, stole the Guru's head and carried it west to the Punjab, for immolation; his body was secretly disposed by Aurangzeb.

It was Tegh Bahadur's son, the next Guru, Gobind Singh, who (no doubt remembering his father's fruitless exercise of combating violence with pacifism) sought to militarize the peaceful Sikh community, saying that when all else failed, it was righteous to pick up the sword. This became the defining ethic of the Punjab: never to submit to oppression, and to actively fight cruelty and injustice.

Such was the homily delivered by the Pundit, who blended his message with the sung words of the Guru. When the last verse was sung, we all rose and bowed, said a parting prayer, and filed out of the temple. I did not stay for the communal meal that follows a Sikh service.

It was early evening now. I had spent the entire day wandering around; I was slowly absorbing what I had read in Raj's journal.

It was as if a portal inside me had opened. I could not name it properly, only that it spoke of solace and joy — and laughter even in the face of adversity — as my grandfather would have said.

That evening, I did not join Raj on the cot for our usual evening chat.

He and Bawa-ji sat for a long time, quietly talking, and frequently laughing.

I was inside the house by the flickering clay-lamp, busy transcribing what I found moving, enjoyable, startling in Raj's journal — a distant world, a far away place, many years ago — a translation of the heart's journey into life.

My lamp began to sputter; from a glass bottle, I added some more mustard oil; the flame strengthened again — an orange tongue that spoke of the promise of sunrise.

Journal Entry: Maps

The peculiar sweet smell of earth after rain, evokes a certain memory, an event that has almost vanished into the namelessness we call history. How many names does history hide?

"Enter into the inner chamber of the mind," says Anselm, "and there seek out the Beloved." He wrote these words for the monks at the Abbey of Bec, which lies not too far from Rouen, just before William conquered England in 1066.

Bec is one of those ruins that fascinate me, scattered through the old forests of Normandy, more eloquent perhaps in their fragmented, overgrown state than they were in their heyday.

It was at Bec that Anselm wrote his works, each one simpler than the first, in which he sought to describe his Beloved. For him, words simply got in the way.

I would often take a rural bus out to Bec or to the nearby ruin of Jumièges, and as I watched the dense forest unwind from a slow green spool outside my window, I came to realize what Anselm had discovered — that words could never describe; they could only name.

It was at Jumièges that the Abbot Robert blessed the banner that William took with him to Hastings. Later, Robert became the Bishop of Canterbury, as did Anselm.

The ruins at Jumièges, were emptier, quieter than Bec's and the stones and the walls echoed nothing more than forgetfulness.

Whenever I went there, I saw an old woman who stood at the entrance, begging. She said nothing; didn't even hold out her hand; and her name has been swallowed by history. Yet for me, the essence of that once proud monastery is preserved in the smell of wet earth, a piece of rough amber, and the story that woman told me one October morning.

Above the ruins, the mist was beginning to dissolve. and an autumnal dampness muffled all sound that came from the nearby road. From the chapel, the voice of monks sang "*vox turturis:*" 'the voice of the turtledove was heard in the land . . . ' There are no monks at Jumièges; it's just a recording — an evocative ploy by the Tourist Board of Normandy.

I gave the old lady a few francs, as I did whenever I came there. She recognized me with a slight nod.

I wandered away from the other visitors and sat on a fallen column, off by myself where the walls became broken stumps and the forest loomed. There were jackdaws circling and calling above the twin turrets that even today are taller than the trees around them. Yet weeds were growing up there, on the topmost stones. How do seeds gain a foothold so high, I wondered.

The leaves were beginning to fall and there was a hush in the air. The apple growers had piled high their pickings on carts by the roadside to my left; the shapes and colours of the mounds were endless. Between the piles, fires had been lit, which in the late morning smoked more than blazed. The sharp smell of burning leaves swirled about.

As I sat in my reverie, I felt a hand on my shoulder. It was the old woman smiling down at me. Then, slowly, deliberately, she sat down next to me and hugged herself into a hunch. I said nothing. Neither did she.

Then, she reached into an inner pocket of her shabby overcoat and took out two deep russet apples. She gave me one, which I accepted with thanks.

She nibbled at hers, while I crunched noisily into mine.

"You are a man, and a man must be different," she said.

What could I say to that?

"Yes, men are different . . . different . . . " she whispered.

I was at a loss. I finished the apple and tossed the core behind me, under the pine trees. The woman put hers back, scarcely touched, in her coat pocket.

I felt awkward in the silence.

"You're always here when I visit Jumièges." I said.

More silence, and then, all at once, she turned to face me.

"Do you know when I was young, a little girl, I imagined that I would see so many far away countries. My father bought me an atlas, and every night before going to sleep, I would turn the page and look at a new country. And when I closed my eyes, I imagined myself in that country, far away, happy, joyous, and thinking of the next destination I'd visit."

This was not the voice of a wretched old beggar. It was eloquent, gentle.

"And do you know, I haven't even been to Paris. I've lived in Jumièges all my life."

I knew I should not interrupt, but I am not sure sometimes whether this talent of mine for listening, for drawing out people's stories, is a gift or an affliction.

"My father and mother were taken away by the Germans during the war," she said. "I don't know why. I was raised by the village priest, who said I would do well if I learned how to cook and clean. I waited for my parents every day to come and take me away, but they never came back. And slowly I got used to living without them, as people do. I lost my atlas, but in my mind's eye, I still remember it was a big book, with dark red covers, like the apples we just ate."

I asked her which country was the one she most wanted to see.

"I don't know the names. I just remember the maps and their colours. I loved the colours. I only knew the countries by their colours. You have travelled much, I think. Do different countries have colours like they show in an atlas?" Her eyes were wide now, and trusting. It was a child that sat beside me.

Yes, I told her, every country was a different colour; you just had to know how to look.

"I thought so . . . I thought so," she said, thankful to have her mythology confirmed.

I was enchanted now. "And what was your favourite colour in that atlas?" I asked her.

"Blue. Yes, blue. Because the countries painted blue seemed like huge seas. And if I looked hard enough, I could see the waves and the ships, and all the beautiful people dancing on the decks."

Her smile was trusting and eager. Her face, I realized, was kind, too — not the twisted, hard look you'd expect from a beggar. But who really is a beggar? For some, life breaks, and nothing will put it together again.

"And do you know when I became a young woman I fell in love, just like you."

There was no love in my life at that time, though there would be very soon, and I've sometimes fancied that old woman could see into the future.

"He was a nephew of the village priest I lived with, and worked for. His name was Lubin. He was from Lillebonne. Yes, I fell in love. And one day, we went into the forest, and in a little clearing, I lay down naked beneath him, and he made me into a woman. That's how men are, you know. They take a child and make her into a woman. And I was happy, so happy, because in his eyes, I saw the sky that shone high above us, from where I thought I saw my mother and my father smiling down at me."

As the jackdaws forayed and cried above us, I took out a small round of Camembert I'd brought with me for lunch. I cut off a wedge, and offered it to her on the point of my pocketknife. Gently, she lifted it off the blade and put into the palm of her hand.

"But you know, sometimes love is not meant to last forever. It wasn't long before the priest found out about us, and he called me a — a whore. Lubin tried to say I was a good girl, but the priest, his uncle, would hear none of it and slapped me hard. He got angrier and angrier, and called me that name many times. He hit me again and again. I cried, asking for mercy, saying I was a poor orphan. He ordered me out of the house that very instant. I begged him to let me stay but he wouldn't listen. My voice, my tears only made him angrier."

She fell silent, staring as if in a trance at the morsel of cheese in her hand. And upon that cheese I saw that two tears had fallen.

I put my arm around her. I felt older than her, almost fatherly. She leaned against me, and her little body shook for some moments in sorrow.

Her face was blotchy now, streaked with thin tears. Reaching into my pocket, I pulled out the cheese and gave her the cloth in which it was wrapped. She took that little piece of cloth and wiped clean her face. I sat holding the cheese, not knowing what to do with it.

She cleared her throat and dabbed at her cheeks again.

"And so I left the priest's house," she went on, in a smaller voice. "What could I do, being but a child? Lubin came with me, and took me to the house of the village schoolteacher, an old man, who drooled and had no teeth. Lubin said he would take me away to Lillebonne that very afternoon. He asked me to meet him here at Jumièges abbey. I was to wait, and he would come, he told me."

I could guess what came next, and almost dreaded to hear it.

"But I stayed with the teacher, who beat me every day, because he couldn't have me as a man should have a woman. He was too weak for that. But instead he beat me, until one day, I hit him back, hard — with a hammer. I hit him on the head until he stopped screaming, and his blood covered the floor, dark red, like the apples we just ate."

She shuddered and slowly wiped her brimming eyes.

"And then the police came, and they took me away and put me in jail, and I stayed there until I grew old. They were going to send me to the guillotine, but the priest, Lubin's uncle, said I didn't deserve to die in that way. Instead, they sent me to jail until I became an old woman. The guillotine might have been better."

I put my arm round her again, but this time she pushed me away. She stood up and walked a few steps, as though I had ceased to exist. But then she turned with that same childlike expression:

"Do you think Lubin will come? He told me to wait here at Jumièges abbey. He said he would come . . . "

Yes, I told her, Lubin would come. One day he would surely come.

She smiled and walked away, wiping her face with the little cloth I'd given her.

The jackdaws had ceased their crying. The ancient turrets reached up, two solitary gestures towards the sky, all meaning battered out of them by the wash of time.

Then I saw, on the ground next to where she'd been sitting, something more yellow than the first fallen leaves there. I picked up this object, rubbing away the dirt. It was a piece of rough amber, clear and deep, with flecks of ancient moss inside. The Romans called amber tears of the gods.

Clutching it in my hand, I went looking for the beggar woman. She was standing again by the gate, looking out at the road. I assumed that the amber was hers, but she looked down at it in surprise when I placed it in her hand.

"It's like my atlas! There are so many maps inside!" she exclaimed, her voice filled with joy.

The air was thick with that scent of earth, wet after rain, and the slow smoke was a wispy wreath around the wooden carts piled high with apples, many the colour of amber.

I wish I had asked her her name.

Journal Entry: Samarkand

Just this morning, I was standing on the Quai du Havre, watching boats and barges glisten in the Seine as they headed to port.

From the Quai I can see all the bridges of Rouen: to my right is Pont Guillaume-le-Conquérant, to my left are Pont Jeanne-d'Arc, Pont Boieldieu, Pont Corneille and, Pont Mathilde. I am thinking how this city has changed me like a lute strewn with delicate purfling that no longer speaks of wood but of sound and the precision of music.

Turning left, I walk up rue Jeanne d'Arc, which bisects the city. By going this way I pass rue du Gros Horloge, with its Renaissance clock tower, beyond which is the Cathedral, and the battle-scarred Palais de Justice. I cross rue Thiers and go to Square Verdrel, which is a tiny, heavily-wooded park, with a tranquil little pond where two cygnets, one black and one white, quietly glide from one end to another. I often find myself here.

During the night, this Square becomes a haunt for prostitutes who lean suggestively against the trees, their faces half-hidden in the darkness, like dreams half-remembered.

I sit on a bench and watch the swans; they come close to the pond's edge, but I have nothing to give them. They quietly paddle on.

Just behind the Square is the Musée des Beaux-Arts, where time and again I am drawn to the gallery on the second floor, to stand before one particular painting. It is Monet's *La rue St. Denis, Fête nationale du 30 juin 1878.* The image is of a jumble of flags: red-white-blue, red-white-blue, over and over again, as if these colours were foliage and flowers bursting from every building. And my eye travels to the very top of the canvas, which shows a sky of light blue. It is there that the resonance lies, the evocation of memory deep inside.

Every time I look at this painting, I enter a labyrinth, whose centre is the blue of my childhood. Is remembrance a ruse?

Once you enter a maze, you must either walk on, or be driven back: only the path matters; there is no revelation, only the belief in a centre.

Since a labyrinth does not begin or end, you need a string to enter it, tied to the outside world. And the colour of this string for me is blue . . .

When I was eleven-years-old, I would go to the Memorial Park, lie down, stare at clouds and dream of so many things. We lived in Wexham, a little village in northern England. Behind me stood a memorial from the Great War: a statue of a soldier in putties, leaning on his rifle, pensive, sorrowing; beneath him were the names of the young men who never came back, who lie in fields far away, beneath green turf, strangers for all eternity — "Lest we forget!"

This park had a high hedge all around it. In the spring my friends and I would find blue robins' eggs in the bushes there, and gently cooing doves.

It was in Memorial Park that I lay on the grass with my very first girlfriend; we were both eleven. I remember she held my hand briefly, as I told her about the travels of Marco Polo, and the many perils of the high Silk Road. She had blonde hair and a cherubic face. Her name was Cynthia.

As a child, I invested names with magic. One such name was *Samarkand*. I don't remember when I first read about this little city in the dusty highlands of Central Asia, but I knew that it was famed for its sweet melons and ripe quinces. If I repeated this name slowly, I would imagine myself on the Silk Road, watching for the minarets of the city, having survived countless hardships, leading my two-humped Bactrian camels, laden with silks and precious unguents. From a distance I would catch a glimpse of the shining domes, deep blue against the pale sky. If I repeated the name again, I would hear antique music, the laughter of happy people, and the shouts of friends who awaited me with open arms, welcoming me home from a perilous journey. In rich-tiled *hamaams*, I would leisurely bathe, and when I emerged, a wonderful repast awaited me of course, with sweet melons and ripe quinces.

Cynthia would listen to my accounts with a wonder-filled face, and when she asked me how blue were the domes of Samarkand, her lips rounded softly. And, with a dashing gesture of my arm that I had learned on the Silk Road, I would tell her the domes were as blue as her eyes.

She and I had a little garden beyond the railroad tracks, where we planted seeds that we had collected from all over. Close to the buttercups would be cucumbers, a lone tomato plant, a spindly unknown trailing vine that seemed on the verge of dying, but never did.

Like far-away distant names, plants, too, were magical; they held a different world. Plants could make you disappear; eat you up and spit out your bones; or lead you to enchanted worlds where good fought against evil. The roots of plants burrowed deep into the dark moist earth, to the deepest depths, where ancient treasure lay, where skeletons mouldered and dragons slumbered, coiled in their fire. And if you were lucky enough to get a seed of a plant that grew tall, you could climb to the top and touch the clouds as they floated by. The best plants were great-domed, tall trees, because if you were being chased by cannibals you could climb really high and be safe in the thick cover of leaves. Of course, cannibals never bothered to climb after you because they couldn't. Their usual practice was to set up camp beneath the tree and wait for you to come down. Little did they realize that you were ready for this siege, and you had laid up a good supply of hard-boiled eggs (my favourite kind of food in those days). At night the leaves kept you warm and you slept beneath the clear light of the eternal moon . . .

Summer seemed endless then, one hot day led to another. We would run across fields, our feet beating a sweet aroma from the ripening clover. And when we were far away from the village, we would veer into pastures where the high grass hid us from view, and we then began to swing imaginary swords, lopping off heads, slaying mythic beasts, and storming steep castles.

Our favourite haunt was a little spring from where our village became a hazy row of steeples and huddled roofs. This spring fed the Wexham pond. Here we would take off our shoes and socks, and let the cold water burble across our toes; it was such a mystery to see a round gush of white water rising from the green sod. While dragon flies flitted around us and blackbirds hopped scolding from one branch to the next, I would tell Cynthia of far away places, always ending with the blue domes of Samarkand. In our minds, we lived not in a little village, but in the enchantment of distant worlds.

When the last haying was done, the entire village smelled of fresh mown fodder, which gave milk its sweetness, I would say. When the fodder was bailed, it was the end of summer and the beginning of autumn.

Then, the wind would become harsher, laden with cold moisture that seeped into our house and ensured that the tip of your nose was forever cold. The fire in the grate would glow red and the coal would give off a hard smell that would last until the spring. Then in mid-October, just before Halloween, the winds would howl and roar, and the rains would come and our streets would be strewn with leaves from all those trees. There was a nip in the air and a briskness in your walk. Everyone would begin raking leaves, each pile a mound of russet or dull brown.

Then leaf-burning would begin: the flare of a single match, quickly buried at the bottom of the pile; at first thin white smoke blown invisible by the wind, and then a thicker billow, until it became a steady blue column; only then could you see the flame as orange as some of the leaves. The bitter reek of that smoke was very distinct, never again to be whiffed until next autumn . . .

Sitting here in Square Verdrel, I can still smell it. The whole of Wexham would be busy burning away this final, unwanted harvest. Every yard had a smoking pile and large circles of ash, which the rains soon made too heavy to be blown about.

The first snow of the year was always a surprise; at first a few flakes floating unnoticeably in the wind, then a steady downfall. I remember seeing this first snow from inside our house, where the coal ranges made the floorboards creak; we would watch the snow while waiting for the bread in the oven! And we would eat hot slices of this bread with butter and honey or cream and jam. When we awoke in the morning to go to school, everything would be white, and our windows ferned with frost. The snow even muffled our shouts and yells during snow-fights, so thickly did it cover all things.

To get to school, we crossed that large field, which only a few months ago had been thick with clover, both white and purple. But now the snow came almost to the top of our Wellingtons. Some days a lone carrion crow would fly above our heads, gripping something dead in its beak. We left our boots in the cloakroom and plodded around in thick socks. Our day began with "God Save the Queen" and the Lord's Prayer.

As the snow piled higher, I would make a haphazard igloo in our tiny backyard with a shovel, despite fingers aching with the cold and my feet numb. It was more a cavern, but to my eyes it looked like an igloo, where I would spend hours on end, fascinated at how blue the roof of snow above my head was thinned almost to a crust by my hollowing. I said that it was blue because snow came from the sky. When I finally crawled out, my knees would be stiff and my nose would hold my breath frozen in hard crystals.

One February day, cold, clear, bright, I was showing Cynthia a squirrel's nest high in a massive pine tree. She didn't seem too interested. I pushed her a little, but she didn't throw any snow in my face; she had a quietness, which turned out to be sadness. When she finally spoke, she said that her family was moving to another village further north; she would be gone by the end of the month. She said her parents had told her that they would bring her to Wexham to visit her friends regularly, though. On her last day, we had a farewell party for her at school, and we sent her off with jam donuts and orange juice. Between the mouthfuls of food, my friends and I were busy impaling any winter-trapped flies we could find on pins and sticking them up on the corkboard where the teacher pinned maps; the idea was to see how long they lived. At the back of our notebooks, we had a sophisticated tabulation system, which told us whose pinned fly lived the longest.

I can't say I missed Cynthia greatly; she is part of those thronging days I call my childhood, from which I sometimes draw out an incident or a face and ruminate how far I've come, how much time I've moved through, for life is a spiraling in love, or an abandonment in the labyrinth at whose centre is the residue of faces, speech of sleeping hands. Some are no more, others forgotten in the bright rustle of dawn . . .

It was just last week in a window of a travel agency on rue de la République that I saw a little poster advertising tours to Central Asia; one of the pictures was a shot of the tombs at *Samarkand*. It looked very desolate, but I was seeing something else. The travel agent came out and asked me if I wanted to come inside and look at their brochures, but I declined.

Here I am, almost a life-time away, thinking of a small English village, a little blue-eyed girl — and the image of that fabled city, whose tales I told her so long ago, is pasted to a window just one street over, here in Rouen.

What became of Cynthia, I wonder? Is she still somewhere in northern England? All the people I grew up with wandered away; none of them stayed on in Wexham. I could walk past her today and we would never know each other; that dreamy girl, that romantic boy vanished behind years . . .

I have been sitting in this Square a long time; it is dusk. The first prostitutes are already here; one smiles demurely at me. I smile back and get up to leave. The cygnets have left the pond and are huddled on the grass; I still regret not bringing them something.

I walk down to Place Maréchal Foch in front of the Palais de Justice where my bus waits, the number 10, which will take me back up to Mont-Saint-Aignan.

Wherever you are, Cynthia, I hope you're happy, and I am sure your eyes are still as blue as the domes of Samarkand, where learned men once fixed stars in their spheres, and where Tamerlane, the Scourge of God, is a pile of bones in his jade tomb, which announces: 'When I arise the world will tremble;' only dust stirs upon the Roof of the World. Scattered are the voices that knew our childhood days, just as the streets of that far away, crumbled, ancient city now house nothing but fallen walls and wind. What do we have but strewn remembrance and half-empty shapes of time?

It was at Samarkand, Cynthia, that the high Silk Road ended for some, for they had seen the world and now yearned for rest . . .

CHAPTER 6

THAT YEAR, THE DUSSEHRA FESTIVAL CAME EARLY IN OCTOBER. A particular bustle rippled through Dhanoa, evidence of the villagers' almost childish joy. The houses were given a fresh coat of whitewash that was brought in from Manali in large solid lumps, which were dumped into a huge barrel of water. It boiled and hissed and gurgled, while the children danced around beside themselves with delight.

Others busied themselves with getting new clothes from the village tailor. It was Hobson's Choice — you could have any style as long as it was the tailor's version of pajama-*kurta* (loose pants and long shirt) for men, or *shalwaar-kameez* (pants and long tunic) for women. Single-handedly he outfitted the entire village in new garments for the festival. He himself never bothered about his own appearance, wearing the rattiest looking pajamas, a faded, wrinkled pale mauve shirt, and a turban so loosely tied that it seemed on the brink of collapsing but somehow never did.

Such was Suraj the tailor, a shriveled little man of about sixty who, at three o'clock sharp in the afternoon, stole out to the back of his little shop, across from the general merchant's store, to puff away at his water-pipe. As a Sikh he was, of course, forbidden the use of tobacco, but this never got in the way of his earnest piety — he put it down to "habit," which the Eternal Guru no doubt would easily overlook. While he was on his smoke-break, the customers just had to wait; none of them grumbled. Suraj was looking after his "habit," they would say with a wink.

When Suraj returned from his water-pipe, everyone pretended that he had gone off to do something else; anything but go off for a smoke. In this way, a harmonious balance was maintained, where the villagers put up with a bad "habit" for new clothes — cut of course to a universal design that made everyone look as though they were wearing the same thing only in different colours.

With whitewashed houses and new clothes, Dhanoa awaited the great festival. Dussehra marks the victory of Rama Chandra, the hero of the epic *Ramayana*, over the demon Ravana, who had abducted Rama's beautiful, golden-haired wife, Sita.

This abduction led to the military expedition against Sri Lanka, Ravana's island fortress. With the clever help of Hanuman, king of the monkeys, Rama survived the repeated setbacks and hardships that faced him. In the end, it was Ravana's own brother who betrayed him, telling Rama where the fortress was the weakest. This was the source of the common saying, *"Ghar da bhedi Lanka dhaae"*, ("an insider destroys Lanka"). Armed with this knowledge, Rama defeated Ravana and rescued Sita. The demon had a huge family and more than a hundred sons, all of whom perished.

Unfortunately, Rama came to doubt Sita's fidelity, and had her burnt on a pyre. This part was left out by the villagers, because it would get in the way of the festive mood. The point was Rama had gone off and rescued Sita — and in the process good had triumphed over evil. Therefore, Dussehra was a festival of lights, when everyone lit clay lamps and placed them on the walls and ledges of their houses, so at night a glow encircled the village making it visible from the farthest field, like a halo that spoke of the victory of light over darkness.

The great day arrived, with a big fair near the apricot grove.

While the women and the children made do with the food and iced sherbets, the men of the village met near the crocus fields and gawked at a fat vat that stood on a trestle.

It had been brought last night by Amarnath, and was filled with fiery *arak*. It must have been at least 80-proof! Amarnath drove a truck for the local grain co-op. He offered a full glass to everyone with a great grin; likely he'd been testing the liquor's strength well before we showed up.

By the time I downed my share, there was already an eager lineup for seconds. But I didn't mind waiting; my eyes were still watering from that first breathtaking draught.

Hard by the apricot grove, a travelling troupe of actors had set up their cart as a stage, draped in gold and red brocade. They had begun enacting select scenes from the Ramayana, with Sita pure as driven snow, Rama and his brother Lakshman both noble and brave, and good old Ravana hamming it up as the vilest villain imaginable, with a wolf-like gait, sneering face, and hungry eyes. The actors didn't use masks, but they did wear costumes copied from the movies.

Poor Sita, how could she possibly withstand such an onslaught of evil, left alone as she was while Rama and Lakshman were off hunting; and the demon appeared to her in the shape of a golden hind, beautiful and beguiling. But we saw the hungry eyes, nor could the lupine gait be so easily hidden.

87

"That's not a deer, Sita!" shouted the children in alarm.

"Don't touch him! That's Ravana!" They screamed again.

But Sita was not listening. And off she went, foolishly chasing after the beautiful hind — only to be seized and carried off to faraway Sri Lanka, where they didn't even speak Hindi, let alone Punjabi.

Soon Rama, his brother Lakshman, and the curly tailed Hanuman were hot on the trail. And it wasn't long before Ravana got his comeuppance, dying rather suddenly after just one blow from the flimsy looking mace, much to the crowd's disappointment. Rama and Sita then did a long song from a popular current film that spoke about their eternal love; it blared from a cassette player, cleverly hidden to one side of the cart.

The play enthralled the children, who immediately began to mimic what they had seen: all the girls were Sitas, and most of the boys were Ramas; of course, some boys pretended to be Ravana and vigorously chased after the girls, routing all the Ramas combined.

The women of the crowd drew moral lessons and muttered them to each other.

"That's what happens when you start casting your eyes around."

"A woman should be happy with what God gives her."

The men were too busy with the *arak* to draw any upright conclusions.

A muddle of laughter, shouts, and screams from the children, and the screechy songs from the cassette player rose like a cacophonous ode to joy over the entire village.

As the sun set, it was time for the great finale, and we all headed for the far bank of the Piplan Nadi, where volunteers had raised a giant, twelve-foot, wood-and-paper figure of Ravana, his ten heads jutting out from his shoulders, five aside. Each face bore menacing, curling mustaches and hideous ogre teeth, painted red and yellow.

"What did Sita see in him anyway?" some women loudly wondered.

The demon was dressed in great sheets of blue and white, donated by Suraj the tailor; these fluttered in the autumn breeze, gusts of which at times threatened to topple the entire figure. But three guy-ropes hung down from Ravana's neck and were tied firmly to wooden stakes.

We waited for the night to fall, when the colossal demon would be set alight and Rama would again be victorious, as he was every year about this time.

With a little, drunken laugh, Raj told me that this was India's *Iliad*.

"Ever the great synthesizer, aren't you?" I said to him, and jokingly pushed him aside.

He laughed and stumbled towards the *arak*. We had just started to make a dent in the vat.

The *arak*'s affect on the men was now evident. Their limbs moved loosely, as they spoke about famous wrestlers, or *pehalvaans*; like the match some years back in Manali between *Dullah pehalvaan* and *Bholu pehalvaan*; someone swore that he heard bones crack when the two wrestlers clashed in the *dangal* (ring) — not that he himself was there, mind you, but a cousin's friend had been the eyewitness.

A few men brought out their *kirpaans* or *talvaar*-swords, and displayed their fencing techniques, which consisted mostly of the slash-and-feint variety. And a group of about twenty men put on a mock battle with quarter-staffs, the preferred weapon of choice of the Punjabi peasant. This group raised a lot of dust, along with clamorous battle-whoops, which were echoed by the boisterous, tipsy audience.

Most of the villagers owned horses, and soon riders were charging up and down the banks of the stream, swords or spears in hand, in a gallant, if sometimes erratic, display of traditional Punjabi horsemanship. No doubt this was the bravura that allowed the Punjabis to subdue the Pathans, a people as belligerent as themselves, chasing them far into the northern reaches of Afghanistan.

A lot of steam was let off that day. It was the first time I had seen Raj deeply happy and laughing. The contagious joy of the festival coloured all of us in its warmth.

The night deepened and the stars lay thick above us, but the festivities were far from over.

The coterie of men drinking got larger and larger. We drank *arak* from steel beakers, and shouted *"Ram Chander di jai"* ("Victory to Rama Chandra") as we took big gulps. I can now safely say that drinking is a national Punjabi pasttime, second only to fighting, of course.

By the time the torch was put to Ravana, there were not too many men standing sober, even the *mahant* wasn't left out. However, Bawa-ji did admonish us with a wagging finger and called upon us to be pious on holy days. We all loudly and heartily agreed with him.

As the flames leaped towards the ten proud heads of the demon, a hush fell over the crowd. This was the great moment: the back of evil was broken.

The fire seethed and roared; became a living, hungry creature. The huge statue began to crumble, and soon fell into a heap of high-shooting flames and leaping sparks. The fire ate up the wood, paper and cloth like a ravenous beast, its howl drowning out the soft gurgle of the Piplan Nadi. The heat washed over us. Each of us stood silent before this primordial being, for we were witnessing an eternal struggle.

With the death of Ravana, the crowd slowly began to dissipate. Mothers held their sleepy-eyed children, while the men drunkenly led off their tired horses. Here and there a sword or a spear glinted in the dying light of the fire.

And Amarnath finally ran out of *arak*.

Raj and I lurched our way home, stumbling on the darkened dirt road, our *arak*-heated blood throbbing at our temples.

Ravana burns bright in the night, the *arak*'s strength burns right down to the gut, the swords glint, the war-whoops are happy, and the charging horses never shy — there may be other Dussehra festivals — but none will equal the one I saw in Dhanoa.

That night, in my drunken haze, I thought I understood why I had wanted to copy parts of Raj's journal — through his journey was I working out my own life?

Journal Entry: Sophie

"Salut!"

A quick peck on both cheeks; a hurried handshake.

And we go our separate ways, promising to be in touch.

The only one missing was Sophie. I haven't seen her for many years now. None of the friends I'd just met could tell me much about her — just snippets.

"Oh, she's in Florence, or maybe Venice."

"But didn't she go to America? Yes, I'm sure she did."

"That was last year. Now she's living in Madrid."

"Our Sophie. She wanted to see the world!"

I walk through rue du Gros Horloge, heading towards the Vieux-Marché.

An exuberant aroma embraces me. The Marché swarms with flower-sellers.

Soaking in plastic buckets of blue, red, green, orange, yellow, is a flood of roses, daffodils, narcissi, tulips, gladioli, ferns, sunflowers, and so many others I cannot name.

In front of me looms the modern Sainte-Jeanne-d'Arc Church; the medieval church, dedicated to another saint, was destroyed in an Allied bombing raid in the last war. The modern church marks the spot where a young girl of nineteen, the holy maid of Domrémy, was burnt alive by the English and the Burgundians.

But I'm thinking of Sophie.

As I wander back to my car, I retrace the six, maybe seven, years to when I first met her. How easily we move from reality to memory. Sometimes I think that only such thoughts hold me here — in this country that forever remains foreign, yet is my home. At times I want to think myself free of this land, and follow the ancient flight of birds to the South. But I have never wanted silence, which is why I am still here. I remember so many faces, so many voices. I know oblivion is never far, for it is like stillness that lies between words. Hours do not merely drip away like the heavy rains of this city — they become life. It is my own face that stares back at me from store windows, and the shadow louring beside me is my own.

I walk all the way down to the Seine and watch its muddy water flow on, unheeding. The barges rock beneath the leaden sky, although the horizon above the hills becomes numinous as standing melody. The water rises and falls as if with the world's breathing.

I think back again to my early years in Rouen when I was living in another very small room on rue de Buffon, just past rue du Lieu-de-Santé . . .

It was mid-winter, and my flat had no heating. My only source of warmth was a hotplate that took ten minutes to boil a cup of water. If I were to define winter gloom, it would be that small room, the grey rain forever thrashing my door and window, and me in my layers of clothes. The only comfort was the brief hot shower early in the morning, and if you were a bit late, the last of the hot water would be gone, not to re-appear until the next day.

In that perpetually cold and damp room, I got into the habit of going to bed early to keep warm and to get up early so I could revel briefly in the warmth of the shower.

Sophie lived in the room above me. I heard her hum as she went up the stairs; and if my door were open, she would duck in to say hello. She smiled easily and laughed joyously. She worked as a beautician, and when she could, she did jazz-ballet.

We were the only occupants of that small house.

In that bleak, grey winter, it was she who gave me warmth.

One night, the rain was especially vicious, lashing, almost clawing at the window. It was well past midnight and I was still awake: my five sweaters and three pairs of socks were not at all conducive to sleep, despite a month or so of practice.

Then my door, always unlocked, slowly opened, and Sophie stuck her head in and asked me to come upstairs for a minute.

I followed her running feet up the steps. I had never seen her room before.

It was warm, tidy, and well-lit.

Could one flight of stairs make all that difference?

"Storms frighten me. And when it rains like this, this house frightens me. You must sleep here tonight, with me." She pouted slightly, and her eyes were timid, like a child's.

I was too frozen to say anything, and closed the door behind me. I heard her laugh softly in her throat when she saw how I was dressed. Self-consciously, I started to peel off my five sweaters.

She took off her housecoat and threw it over a chair.

"What are you really doing in Rouen?" It seemed an ambiguous question.

"I don't really know," I said, struggling now on one foot to remove my extra socks. "I've asked myself the same question."

I switched feet, leaning against the wall for support.

"I believe I'm hoping to find something."

I think my answer amused her, or perhaps it was my awkward fumbling about with my clothes, for she smiled, took my hand and led me to bed — a nest of soft blankets and pillows that breathed out a floral perfume. She pulled the blankets around us, chattering on as casually as if we were sitting in a café. She told me she had travelled to the States a lot; she liked the country because everything had filmic proportions.

"The oddest thing is going to the cinema there, because when you come out, everything looks the same as the world you've seen on the screen. In that way, I think it's easier watching American films in France; at least you can tell what is real and what isn't when you come out of the cinema."

I was too busy burying myself in the enormous warmth of the bed to come up with a proper response.

"You know," she said, her face close to mine, with a look of mock gravity, "you have gone too far into yourself. You must come out. This is not good."

This late night philosophy was something I was not prepared for. And I merely looked at Sophie, with her light brown hair and dark eyes. Then she gently held my face in her hands and said nothing.

The warmth of her body was far richer than that of her bed, and the fragrance of her skin was a soft cocoon over me. Her eyes were hazy with expectation as I kissed her; she laughed deep in her throat, and her arms pulled me up into the surety of her golden body.

As she lay sleeping beside me, I gently touched her neck and put my lips to where her pulse beat slow. Outside, winter rain washed cloudless some ancient skin of memory, so that morning broke white and clear upon our window . . .

I am on rue Vicomte; this is where my car's parked.

Smiling to myself, I wonder what Sophie is doing right this minute.

I have not thought of her in months, but today her face is before me continuously.

Yes, the only reason why I came to meet these friends was that I thought Sophie would be among them.

If truth be told, I came to meet only her . . .

Who delights in your dancing, now that I am gone? Who praises the beauty of your stride? Who will give you immortality in this world? Would you were walking on the shore by the sea, and I was an eager breeze that in blowing by parted your blouse and gently caressed your breasts. There will be some who will remember us when we are gone. I spend many hours walking unfamiliar paths, my mind broken like a hunted beast. Can searching last forever? You have nothing to tell me, nothing to say. Seasons will come and go and years will vanish into decades. Nothing lasts forever, not even song, for pain turns all things to stone. I am bound by breath, my sadness yet lies unspoken. I crouch like growth untamed, thinking of your fragrant skin like dew rinsed from the immortal sky. Dawn is a boat that rests by the shore, certain neither of night or day. Do not forget the rivers churning beneath a gauze of mist; these are the rivers that hold wisdom at their confluence, that flow past silent hours and bring us to conclusion — these you have sought; and without rivers the seas would be empty, as my heart is without you. My words have no memory; they have knowledge only of you. My life is your description, and my dreams the grammar of desire, for existence cannot be without desire, as stars love the sky, trees love earth, night loves the moon, as songs balance iron. I know the secret of the sun is darkness: colour's end. Even chaos in the end teaches order. How have you become my joyful wisdom, my holy secret: the sight of your breasts could disarm my cunning; the flow of your hair could teach me patience. Do you know how eager my heart is, even now, how changeless my yearning? Come, look at the brightness of my eyes submerged in the sky, the up-turned bowl, beneath which we move, ever planning our tomorrows. Is God still on his throne of silence? When you walk, think of me; do not step too far away, even as the slow morning drips on ravaged walls and cracked flower-pots — the heart can only remember itself: for what is poured remains beautifully empty . . .

Slowly, I drive up the mountain to Mont-Saint-Aignan, thinking of all the things I have to do today.

But as soon as I get home, I am rummaging through old papers; I am looking for a packet of letters sent to me from the U.S., Italy, Egypt. Finally, in a dusty cardboard box, I locate the bundle. I draw off the thin, blue elastic band that holds the envelopes together, and take out the first letter.

Inside are memories, lived moments, the excitement of new places, new people. Every sentence is a signature of Sophie's joy and pleasure, her laughter and delight. How fresh her writing looks, how fresh the paper still, as if she sent the letter yesterday, and not these many years ago.

How many faces we meet, how many hearts? And how many can we still name in the rush of years?

At the very bottom of the box, I find two more pieces of paper. They aren't part of a letter; and now I can't remember when she gave them to me. But the writing is hers: I can see her, with her deep blue fountain pen in hand, bent over a pad of paper, and she writes . . . "Meditations in Vermont in Winter":

I.
Three russet rosehips, snow in late afternoon:
thickets draped with twilight.
This withering sun, the haze of curtains,
specks of pigeons, and wind,
like Nineveh the golden,

97

where reed barques sat deep
in the musk-harbouring Tigris

II.
Blank, round sky, the precision of comets:
I was not there.
Some tongue-hooded stars,
and Alexander, Abelard and Astrolabe died.
I was not there.
Babble of Babylon.
Dust, but no gardens:
I was not there.

III.
I cannot transform these last snowflakes
like the hollow of your throat
I have nothing to remember:
water in your palm.
Again there is this straw-pale moon
which we have stared at for ages
and this empty, chanting wind

IV.
Your hand will never wipe away
the moments I have distanced.
Infinity has no meaning
like light years trailing stars.
Walk with me softly
across this foot-imprinted field,
guessing the faces beneath.

Carefully, I refold the two pages and bind again the
letters with the fraying elastic band.

In some way, with Sophie I began to see why life unfurls as it must. Before I met her I was formless, caught in a web of vagaries. I was like breath, which must be brought in and then brought out, changed. She transmuted me. When Sophie took me inside her, I felt that our joining thwarted forgetfulness and solitude.

In the end, how gently we let go of the world when the time comes, as though our link is nothing more than gossamer quickly broken by a sudden rush of wind.

Do you still have graceful thoughts, Sophie? Is the world still one long joyous morning for you?

Perhaps next summer you will come visit Rouen from wherever you are; and perhaps we will meet for coffee on a bright afternoon, and talk until the shadows are deep and thick all around us; and perhaps we will walk together to my car, and your laughter will echo in the night, and your words will bring me warmth as you once did on that cold, damp night, when the storm in its anger would not let you sleep . . .

CHAPTER 7

WHAT DOES IT MEAN TO LIVE IN TWO WORLDS? Or perhaps even three or four? Raj's journal suggested a man who was comfortable in any land, unburdened by the baggage of a particular culture. Perhaps it is good to know that your home is not linked to your race, but to the land that offers you contentment. Some may call this naïve. Not even the Punjab was a homeland for Raj; genetically he belonged; spiritually he lived in the community of the world.

This, too, Raj taught me — before, I was lost in the fog race and ethnicity, and all the strife that it has engendered.

One day, as we walked towards the village late in the afternoon, Raj spoke about his stay in Germany and Italy. Again, his words gave flesh to names, and his descriptions animated the places he had once seen — perhaps even called "home." It was the atmosphere of a land that made him stay on. Germany was a land obsessed with order and cleanliness; while Italy was just too busy living to develop such obsessions— it was a bacchanalian land, ancient yet utterly modern, degenerate yet pure, raucous yet restrained. It had learned to live in the fertile tension between these opposites. This naturally suited Raj. East and West struggled within him; and he did not choose between the two. He did not need a cultural crutch to give himself meaning and definition; neither did he use his race to bludgeon others with. Raj ground no axes, nor was life a political act — it was a search for symmetry, harmony, happiness, and perhaps even redemption.

How strange it was to hear his cadenced French, like an exotic bird whose origins none can point to, though all who see it marvel at its rare plumage or unique call.

In some way, Dhanoa was Raj's cage. He was the odd man of the village, ridiculed by some, befriended by most. It was true that he had grown up in *Vilayat*, the generic term for the West that the villagers used, which literally meant England. *Vilayat* was a place that no one in the village could even dream of seeing; thus to have someone among them, a man, who had not only seen *Vilayat* but had lived there as well, was in some way a matter of pride. But *Vilayat* was also the cause of the ridicule directed at Raj — for only a fool would leave such a place and come to live in Dhanoa. Why not go to Chandigarh, or New Delhi even? His family was not from Dhanoa, the villagers observed; they were city folk. But which city? No one knew. Perhaps he was a great criminal in *Vilayat* and was hiding out in Dhanoa. Here somebody would interject with the remark that if he were such a criminal, the police would have nabbed him a long time before, and not let him live peacefully. Did not the people of *Vilayat* have long arms that could reach anywhere in the world? Look, they had even gone and walked on the moon. None could dispute the obvious logic of this interjection. But doubt persisted, since no one could explain satisfactorily why anyone in his right mind would leave *Vilayat*.

We had gone to the village to buy kerosene and as we walked back, we called out to Bawa-ji, beneath the walnut tree, to come and take afternoon tea with us. Half an hour later he joined us.

Like the villagers, we drank tea out of thick glasses, with plenty of milk and sugar. It was difficult to hold a hot glass without the aid of a handkerchief. Bawa-ji used the dangling end of his long scarf. As we drank the hot, sweet liquid, he began to tell us a little about himself.

He was born in Kabul, Afghanistan, where his family had lived for centuries, carrying on trade as cloth merchants. They brought dyes from Lahore and tinted great lots of cotton cloth in huge vats. In the fields just outside the city walls, the fabric would be slung out on long ropes to dry in the high sun. On dye-days, once a week, there were countless rows of blues, reds, yellows, greens, oranges, and pinks — colours most popular for *basant*, or the spring festival. This cloth was then marketed in the family's own stores, which could be found all over the North West Frontier Provinces, even as far as Isfahan and Tehran in Iran. Every store bore the same name: "Rangarang", which means "Colours upon colours".

By April, in Kabul, the snow would start to melt on the Shahr Darwaza Mountains that faced the ancient city, and the melt-water would flow down in scurrying rivulets, feeding the great Kabul River, which seemed to go mad, surging and swelling, as if exulting in the sudden retreat of winter.

It was in April, too, that the schools opened; they were closed for three months in winter.

On the first day of school, there were hundreds of children, boys and girls, in great flocks, like the returning cranes and geese in the bright sky above, boisterously rushing to class, all dressed in fresh, new clothes, all carrying light khaki canvas satchels.

It was in the months before school that business was best for Rangarang.

Bawa-ji still spoke good Farsi and Pashto, the two languages of Kabul, which he said, with a sad little smile, were his mother tongues; Punjabi was only a third language that he would speak occasionally when he visited Lahore with his parents.

"I still think in Pashto; and my dreams are in Pashto, or sometimes Farsi; never in Punjabi," he said wistfully. He did speak Punjabi with a Pashto accent.

He talked about his father, Wasava, who was a good friend of Shah Amanullah Khan Ghazi, who later became the king of Afghanistan, after the British created a buffer zone between themselves and the Russians with the Treaty of Rawalpindi in 1919. Wasava knew Amanullah when he was merely an Emir (nobleman) and not yet a Shah (king). They became good friends through their great love of hunting.

"My father and Amanullah would go off with a party of men and spend several months each summer just hunting, following game to various pastures and feeding grounds. Of course, this was before my father got married. He was a very good shot with a gun; much better in fact than Amanullah, though Amanullah was the better horseman. He had a beautiful bay mare that he rode, whose tail he himself carefully braided."

As far as Bawa-ji could remember, his family had lived in Kabul, perhaps from the time of the Hindushahi, long back when Hindu kings ruled Kabul from the eighth to the tenth centuries AD.

It was upon the sudden death of Bawa-ji's grandfather that Wasava was asked by his mother, a strong matriarch, to stop being a boy and become a man and take over the family business. Sadly, Wasava put away his rifles, his jodhpurs, his special riding boots, and took on the duties of a householder and a businessman. Amanullah also settled down, becoming a Shah of modern Afghanistan in 1926: a glorious new country for a bright new century.

Of course, Amanullah saw less and less of Wasava now, but they occasionally wrote to each other, discussing, as if they were still young and footloose, how plump the quails were that year, or what route the wild deer might take in their slow migration South.

This connection with the royal household continued with Bawa-ji, who was born in 1930; he was a personal friend of Muhammad Zahir Shah, the last king of Afghanistan, who was deposed in 1973. Bawa-ji was a frequent guest at the royal palace in the Dar-ul-Aman district, which meant "the door of peace:" the section of Kabul where stood many Deco buildings, the abodes of the rich. It was in fact with Bawa-ji's help that Zahir Shah slipped into India via Pakistan, after he was deposed, and made his way eventually to Italy. He had wanted Bawa-ji to come with him, but Bawa-ji had another calling; so they parted friends, never to see each other again.

What kind of magnet was Dhanoa, I wondered, that it attracted the likes of Bawa-ji and Raj? These men who had seen so much of the world were now content to sit beneath a walnut tree and either teach a handful of children or meditate. I looked at them both, tranquilly sipping their tea, and could not begin to explain them. Though years apart, they were similar in many ways. Both were outsiders to India, and yet were extremely Indian. They did not seem attached to any land, really; citizens of the world, they were happy in Paris or Madrid, in a king's hunting lodge or palace, or here on a little, wooden cot, placed against a coarse mud wall. Golden kings, and golden princes must come to dust . . .

When he was sixteen, Bawa-ji enrolled at Kabul University to study mathematics. That first year was a fateful one: 1947. Rumours were thick that the English were quitting India after more than two hundred years. By August, these rumours were a reality: the English created Pakistan, a separate land for Muslims, by slicing up the Punjab and Sindh. There was panic in the Hindu and Sikh communities of West Punjab. This panic was felt as far north as Kabul, since most Hindu and Sikh families there had relatives in the soon-to-be affected areas. Many hurried down to get family members out — those that had the means, of course. Stories came from Lahore of mass exits, of people frantically trying to move east, of impending slaughter.

Bawa-ji's uncles both lived there, in Lahore — the city where Kipling lived and edited *The Civil and Military Gazette*, and where his father, Lockwood, painted and designed buildings, like the Museum. The old city was also the last home of the Koh-i-Nur diamond; it was a place renowned for culture, the arts, music, learning.

Bawa-ji's father hurried down to Lahore to make sure his two brothers and their families didn't linger, hoping for the trouble to blow over; the rest of his family were either in Afghanistan or Iran. He and his brothers headed for New Delhi, where most of the migrants from West Punjab ended up. Seeing them safe, he made for Peshawar, just as communal unrest was starting, to fetch his wife's family.

When the riots broke out, they came with the severity of a Punjabi dust storm that turns the sky an angry red. That summer, people say, the sky was perpetually red, not from the dust storms, but because of the blood that flowed.

Bawa-ji's mother's family was not so lucky. When Wasava reached them, the riots had gained momentum, each day brought greater slaughter — Hindus and Sikhs killing Muslims, and Muslims killing in turn.

Since there were no airplanes out of Peshawar, the family had to take the train — wisely they chose to travel north, rather than east — for the trains that headed east were soon called *Mort Gaddian*, "Death Trains," because all the passengers would arrive slaughtered, women, children, old people, young people, everybody; only the train driver would be spared so he could drive the train out of the new Pakistan, the "Land of the Pure," which had no room for Hindus or Sikhs.

By the time the riots ended sometime in the autumn of 1947, only half-a-percent of Hindus and Sikhs were left in all of Pakistan; before 1947 they constituted almost half the population. There were communal riots in Bengal as well, which was split up and called East Pakistan; but none of these areas saw the sustained ferocity, the "ethnic cleansing" that the Punjab did.

Age-old hatreds resurfaced, consuming whole families, entire villages. Some estimate that more than two million in the space of three months were slaughtered; others say more. No one knows; no one will ever know.

Most Punjabi families were affected by this bloodletting. 1947 was supposed to be a year of "freedom," of "self-rule," the end of colonialism under two centuries of British rule. And this new freedom, *Azaadi*, would herald a new age, a new Indian man, who would be both modern and traditional, a controller of his own destiny, equipped with a finer mentality than the subservient one of his fathers. 1947 would be a year of new beginnings.

But for more than two million people in the Punjab — Hindu, Sikh, Muslim — that great day, that new era, never dawned. They were hacked, stabbed, bludgeoned, drowned, burnt, gang-raped, mutilated into oblivion. The sky was blood-red every evening that summer. When would this calamity end, people asked? This had never happened when the English ruled. Why now?

In 1947, it was common to find fingers, hands, penises, legs, breasts, feet, women's braids lying about on the streets and by the sides of roads, tossed away like refuse, unwanted flotsam on the great sea of "India's freedom."

1947. A year of blood for the Punjab. One more genocide in a long series of genocides — it isn't for nothing that the Punjab is also called "the battlefield of India." And India's freedom was fought out relentlessly on the Punjab's plains. The long-awaited *Azaadi* translated into rows and endless rows of corpses piled twenty or thirty high. No one could give them a proper cremation or burial.

"The pariah dogs were very well fed that year," sighed Bawa-ji.

Raj was on his feet; he went to the door that led out from the courtyard; he leaned against the jamb.

Then he turned to face us, cocked his head to one side, and said in a voice that was no more than a whisper.

"My father was the only survivor from a family of ten brothers and sisters who lived in Rawalpindi."

His father was luckily in Bombay studying, when Partition came, and could not make it back to Rawalpindi; there were no trains, and travel by foot was suicide. Daily he waited at the Amritsar train station; his parents, brothers and sisters, cousins, uncles and aunts, a family clan of about fifty people —never emerged from the ravaging of West Punjab.

"To his dying day, my father wondered what happened to his family. That knowledge was denied him. To his dying day, he cursed Gandhi and Nehru. Isn't it ironic that Gandhi owes his message of non-violence entirely to Tolstoy? My father went back to Rawalpindi, now Pakistan, in the late '60s, from England; but there was nothing to be found, nothing to go back to. Even the family home that overlooked the River Lye, had long vanished."

While we were talking, Amarnath the truck driver had come into the courtyard. His huge figure stood quietly listening 'til Raj had finished, but then he let out a great sigh and stepped forward.

We made room for him on the cot.

A story will breed a story, and Amarnath had his own to tell.

He was a great bear of a man, more than six feet tall, who spoke loudly, no matter what the occasion, but he used his words frugally. No doubt his long days on the road by himself in his truck had conditioned him to say little. He cleared his throat before he spoke.

In 1947, Amarnath was a six-year-old boy, living with his father, Niranjan, in Gujranwala, West Punjab. They were a poor family and did not have the means to leave the city on the train, as had most of the well-to-do Hindus and Sikhs two weeks earlier. Father and son would have to undertake the great trek east on foot, with a group of similar migrants. This poorer folk had only a few bullock-carts between them, which they piled with hastily tied armloads of belongings.

Niranjan had gotten up very early that morning and gathered everything in an easy-to-carry cloth bundle; he was eager to be off since the one-room that he rented belonged to a Muslim merchant; and day-by-day more and more non-Muslims were being slaughtered openly in the city.

On that mid-August morning, before the sun arose, Niranjan recited the *Japji*, or morning prayer, while he donned the conventional *shastras* (weapons): long sword, a short dagger, a thin steel lance, and a *dhaal*, a round iron buckler that he slung over his back.

Amarnath was an only child, whose mother had died in childbirth. Father and son looked after each other. They were both used to hardships; but this was different. The earlier crises had been financial: the struggle to make ends meet. Now, it was a matter of life and death. Niranjan might have to do what he had never done before in his life — kill others, so he and his son could live.

Little Amarnath was now awake and he watched his father tie two hard, leather slippers on the top of his head, over which he tightly wound his deep green turban, the long end of which he let dangle over his chest.

Their room was completely bare; when Amarnath had gone to sleep their few possessions lay around him. But now all was gone. It no longer seemed the same place.

His father gave him some cool *lassi* and bread from last night, and told him to get ready. Amarnath sensed his father's urgency, and hurriedly put on his little pajama-*kurta*. Normally, in the morning he went to the school in the Sikh temple. But not today. The sun wasn't even up yet.

Before Amarnath could finish the bread, Niranjan took him by the hand, and swung the bundle of belongings over his left shoulder. He was a big man, known for his strength through all of Gujranwala. He could toss two hundred pound sacks of wheat as one flings pillows on a bed; and he could knock down a full-grown bull; but this he would do only occasionally when pressed by boisterous friends, and when he'd had a few drinks.

Father and son hurried through the still-dark streets, and before long they were at the new market-square, which stood outside the old city walls.

A crowd of migrants had gathered there, eager to be off before the Muslims awoke. The men wore somber expressions, the women cried.

Niranjan heard the fearful whispers, the anger, the incomprehension.

"Why do we have to leave our own homes like thieves in the night?"

"Who dreamt up this madness?"

"Where is Gandhi and his stupid hunger strikes?"

"Where is Nehru?

"We're just ordinary people. No one cares what happens to us."

Someone laughed wryly and muttered, "It's on the backs of the poor that great men build their dreams."

Niranjan listened to this talk, but he himself stood silent, clutching the hand of his little son, who was nearly asleep on his feet.

Most of the people knew each other, and a few of them made sure that all were present and accounted for before they commenced their march eastward.

"If anyone gets left behind, they'll have to fend for themselves," came the whisper.

The chances of surviving alone, surrounded by Muslims, were slim; unless one converted to Islam.

Just two days before, in this same marketplace, the Muslims had corralled three hundred destitute Hindus and Sikhs and "converted" them, forcing them to eat beef, and circumcising many of the younger men. There was no one to come to their aid, no one they could turn to. God himself had turned His face from them.

Any hope of surviving in Gujranwala had evaporated.

The calm of the twilight mocked the group's urgency, but the air was already close; it would be a very hot August day.

A few men turned to Niranjan.

"You were the last non-Muslims in the city. We thought you weren't coming, or dead."

Niranjan said nothing; stood stoically silent.

Paro, the wife of Iqbal Chand, Niranjan's childhood friend, took little Amarnath in her arms and placed him in the cart in which she rode; the couple had no children of their own. Child that he was, Amarnath was soon asleep again in Paro's arms.

It was decided that the children would ride in the bullock-carts with as many of the women and old people as possible. The men would circle the carts for protection.

The huddled caravan headed out, eastwards, to a land that none had seen, towards India, which they were told was their true homeland — not here in Gujranwala, where their forefathers had lived since time immemorial.

"Who dreamt up this madness?" someone again muttered.

Amarnath let out another great sigh. His shoulders stooped, his great hands clenched on his knees. He rose from the cot, and began to pace about. His face was awash with pain.

"These are hard memories, my friends. We had to leave our home, our city, because it no longer belonged to us. We were told that we would be given land in eastern Punjab. But for us who had no land or property to begin with, there was nothing. It's a good thing that many were cut down as we ran; at least they didn't have to become foreigners here."

His swept out his arms as if to encompass all of Dhanoa; perhaps all of eastern Punjab, and India beyond.

"Look at me! I don't have a homeland." Amarnath nearly shouted; anger had replaced sorrow.

Bawa-ji nodded.

Raj and I said nothing, but watched the towering man pace in front of us. He seemed compelled, though, to finish his story.

It was with a muffled rush that the caravan scrambled away from the city. Many turned back and looked with tears at their homes; others urged them to stop dawdling and just keep moving.

And as the fearful migrants cleared the city limits, dawn broke through the sky.

Steps quickened; bulls were pushed into a speedy gait; women softly cried into their *chunni*-scarves. With the cover of darkness gone, the cloud of dust rising behind them could easily be seen from the city walls.

A sound of beating kettledrums began to follow the group.

The incessant rhythm was like a racing heartbeat, soon interspersed with shouts of *"Ya! Ali! Allah-u-Akbar!"* ("O Ali! God is great!"), the Muslim battle-cry.

The men moved nearer the creaking carts; the women clasped the children closer.

The climbing sun began to heat the air.

The drums and the bellowing, *"Ya! Ali! Allah-u-Akbar!"* chased the fleeing men, women and children, drawing closer like hounds catching up to prey.

There was nowhere to run — an insignificant column of people trudging desperately eastwards, alone in the wide, dusty plain.

Niranjan rallied the men.

"We can't outrun them. Let's stand and fight. And if we die, at least it will on our native soil. Why should we give up our homes without a fight?"

"How can we fight them? We have a whole city chasing us. It'll be suicide if we fight."

But some agreed with Niranjan.

The battle cry and the drums were almost upon them.

Niranjan ran over to the cart where Paro and Amarnath huddled; he gave the woman his steel lance, telling her to stay low in the cart, among the bedding, and to jab any Muslim face that drew near.

With that he rushed off to the rear of the caravan, where the other men stood fearfully clustered.

There was no longer any debate as to whether they should run or fight; the choice had been made for them.

A mass of Muslims was dashing towards them; scythes, quarterstaffs, knives, swords, axes, spears jabbed the early morning air. Faces sweaty, hard, fierce, angry, livid came into view.

The drums stopped, along with the battle-cry.

Then, another shout was heard in the mob:

"Sareh kafir, murdabad! Ya! Ali! Allah-u-Akbar!" ("Death to all infidels! O Ali! God is great!").

The entire mob now shouted as one.

Niranjan stood with the men, who numbered no more than eighty, most of whom didn't have weapons, other than the ubiquitous quarter-staff. Only the Sikhs among them carried swords; and more than half of these were frail old men.

With a loud voice, Niranjan gave the Sikh call to battle, used from the time of Guru Gobind Singh, when he fought the Muslims.

"Jo boleh, so nihaal. Sat Sri Akaal!" ("Blessed are they who say, 'True is the Immortal One'").

A quavering chorus of voices, Hindu and Sikh, joined him in this call.

Niranjan drew his sword, given him by his father, who had received it from his father; it was said to date from the time of Guru Gobind Singh, who had blessed the blade as wondrous. Indeed, it was Gobind Singh who had given God a new epithet, *Sarbloh*, meaning, "He who is all steel," which referred to God's sword of justice.

Niranjan prayed God to brace his sword-arm, so he could fight the demons before him.

Women began to weep loudly and called upon God to be merciful and to forgive their sins.

Their prayers were answered by a louder, fiercer shout from the Muslims who were upon them.

Amarnath, now awake, trembled in Paro's arms; she covered the child in the bedding and the bundles, and then gripped the lance grimly, with both hands.

The mob surged around the huddled eighty men. Niranjan recognized some as personal friends.

All that was over.

The slaughter started soon thereafter.

There was no more time for fear.

He and Amarnath had to survive.

"Sareh kafir murdabad! Ya! Ali! Allah-u-Akbar!"

Niranjan drew a sharp breath and struck the first Muslim that rushed at him, brandishing a sickle.

The sword sliced through the man's right shoulder; he gave a wretched scream and feel to his knees, his blood sputtering bright upon the earth.

Then Niranjan struck at another man who came at him with a lance, giving him a side-slash through the midriff.

Then came another. Niranjan side-stepped and struck the man square on the neck. The blade was true, and the man's head rolled in the dust.

Niranjan was mobbed. He felt himself go into battle-fury. Was this what the Guru spoke of, when he described the ancient heroes in battle?

Niranjan's sword-arm stood him in good stead, though his face was spattered with gore, and the pommel of his sword was slick. He struck, parried, hacked and slashed — all the while shouting at them to stop.

Iqbal Chand, who was short and slim, stood close to Niranjan. There were tears running down his cheeks, as he thrust and jabbed with a short pitchfork he'd picked up from somewhere; he hit no one, but his efforts kept the attackers at bay.

Of the eighty men, less than a dozen were still on their feet.

Groans and cries filled the air; blood and mangled limbs littered the earth.

The Muslims now began to attack the carts, dragging off the old people, the women and the children, slashing furiously at each body they pulled down. The pitiful whimpers of infants did not stop the assailants' blood-lust; mothers begged hopelessly.

When Niranjan saw the carnage of children, a fresh rage overtook him. A roar escaped his lips, as he gripped his sword with both hands and swung at the faces that kept coming at him — faces that he once greeted with a smile in the busy bazaars of Gujranwala.

He felt blows to his head; the hard, old slippers kept him from injury.

115

The fury of his attack made the mob hesitate briefly.

Niranjan dragged Iqbal Chand away. He was looking for the cart in which were Paro and Amarnath.

All around him were women's cries and children's screams of incomprehensible terror.

Muslims were yanking children from their mothers' arms and either smashing their brains out against the cart wheels, or tossing them into the air, then spitting the newborn and the toddlers on their pitch-forks, spears, or sickles — all the while encouraging each other with words like:

"Brothers, God will reward us in heaven for killing his enemies. *Kafirs* have no souls, like animals! Kill them all!"

Niranjan screamed out Amarnath's name, and ran faster. He could not find the cart.

In the swirling dust he could not tell one cart from another.

He was still holding on to Iqbal Chand, who was pitifully crying out to God for mercy.

Then he saw Paro, covered in blood, standing in her cart, gripping the lance he had given her, grimly thrusting at the Muslims around her.

Niranjan let go of Iqbal Chand, gave another roar, and rushed at the milling attackers.

He hewed and slashed with his sword; the blade biting through necks, backs, shoulders, faces, upraised hands and arms.

Blood sprayed his face and clotted in his long beard; streams of sweat stung his eyes.

Blindly he struck whoever came near him. Truly his sword was blessed by the Guru; it did not fail him. His shield rang on his back from blows he could not see.

Iqbal Chand, seeing his wife surrounded, was like a man possessed. He no longer called out to God; his pitchfork was slick with blood.

The dust swirled around them.

Amarnath fell silent again; he put both hands to his face and sat heavily next to me. When he spoke, his voice was scarcely audible.

"I can still hear the screams of pain, the stuttered shouts for mercy, and that peculiar painful moan when a man receives the first blow. All the while I was bundled up, stifling in the heavy blankets and bundles, afraid to move, afraid to breath, lest they find me."

The attack lasted perhaps twenty minutes, but to Niranjan it seemed everlasting.

The dust obscured the horror all around.

Niranjan lowered his sword. No one was attacking him.

He wiped his face with his sleeve. None of the men that stood with him was alive. They were all gone.

He stood gaping in a daze at the confusion of battered, mutilated bodies of the old, women, children, men.

Such was the ritual of slaughter in 1947.

The fight was over; the Muslims had won.

Of all the people that started the journey just an hour or so back, only Iqbal Chand and Paro, Niranjan and Amarnath were still alive — along with a few young women whose tribulations now began.

First, the Muslims herded these women into a group and tore off their clothes.

Then standing in a circle around them, they spat on the women, whose tears flowed in helpless anger, fear, shame.

Within the hour, they had lost their parents, brothers, husbands, children.

117

A merciless death was next.

After the ritual of spitting, the Muslims threw the women down and the rape began.

Their screams of agony floated up to the empty sky, never reaching New Delhi, where Nehru was now Prime Minister of India; nor did Gandhi, the great-soul, hear the women of Gujranwala, busy as he was with a new batch of homespun.

Tears burst from Niranjan as he saw a group of men take turns raping a young girl of fourteen, at whose birth Niranjan had danced in joy. She was the daughter of an old friend. He could now do nothing to help the young girl. He had to save his own son.

Some Muslims, who were waiting their turn with the women, were busy lopping off the penises of all the dead men and sticking them in the mouths of other corpses; this job they called "circumcising the infidel bastards," who were a burden on God's good earth.

Amidst the dust and confusion, Niranjan and Iqbal Chand grabbed the bull that surprisingly had not been killed or taken away, and pulled at the cart. The bull began to trot, happy to be away from all the bedlam; Niranjan pulled harder, helping the animal.

The four survivors left that place of slaughter, under cover of dust.

At the first public well, Niranjan removed his turban, washed away the gore, and then, with Iqbal Chand's help, cut off his long hair and shaved off his beard, with his sharp knife. He could no longer be recognized as a Sikh. He also cut off Amarnath's long, braided hair.

As they headed further east, they posed as a group of Muslims, and whenever they passed a village, Niranjan and Iqbal Chand made sure to pull back their foreskins, little Amarnath's too, so they would look circumcised and pass as Muslims.

This trick saved their lives several times. Each mob they met ordered them to recite the *Kalma* (the Muslim creed), which they did: *"La-illaha-il-lallah; Muhammad rasul-lillah"* ("There is but one God, and Muhammad is His prophet").

And just to make sure, the mob made them pull down their pajamas. The bared glans saved their lives; they were told to be on their way and to kill any uncircumcised *kafirs* they found.

Paro never spoke throughout the long journey; she merely held little Amarnath and hummed him gently to sleep.

It took them nearly two weeks to reach the border and finally cross into India, their new homeland.

Amarnath cleared his throat and ran his hand over his face.

"In time, my father and Iqbal Chand set up a taxi-stand in New Delhi; we prospered modestly; my father is still alive and cannot forget that he had to become a murderer because of politicians' promises. Paro did not survive in her new home; she missed Gujranwala too much, and the slaughter affected her in a different way."

Amarnath touched his right temple.

"She who was always laughing, now spoke very little. She died in 1950. Poor Iqbal Chand carried on with my father, both of them widowers. He died just last year, in his sleep."

Amarnath rose, and went to stand in the doorway.

We sat in silence.

119

The nightingales in the walnut tree began their song, and the wind picked up, ruffling the wheatfields, stirring through the crocuses.

Bawa-ji broke in, speaking softly, gently.

"It wasn't the Muslims that killed us — it was the mob, which has neither a face nor a creed. Yes, I am angry, but I will never direct my anger towards a man because he calls God by a different name — such has been India's long history. And we still haven't learned anything. Look at us."

"You are right." Amarnath's big voice was itself again, his words boomed out into the evening.

"No, I don't hate Muslims. Why should I? They're like me. Our Guru taught us to see all men as brothers. And besides, they too suffered in 1947. We spilled their blood; they spilled ours. There's no difference between us. We're all the same."

Raj looked at me and smiled sadly.

"When we start living in tribes and groups — the result is 1947. We should forget who we are, but not what we are. We're not Hindus and Muslims, Punjabis or not. We're humans — we live and we die, no matter who we claim to be. Is that not so, Bawa-ji?"

The *saddh* nodded.

"Yes, only by forgetting can we learn a new wisdom."

The song of the nightingales grew louder.

Raj, Amarnath, and I decided to get some supper; we asked Bawa-ji to join us, but he declined, saying that it was his fast day.

We left him on the cot, and we heard him begin the ancient Sanskrit chant: *"Om bhu, bhuv, swaha* . . . ("I praise God who is earth, who is air . . . ").

In the village before us, points of light shone like beacons.

Journal Entry: Christine

At night this city changes: one Rouen sleeps, while another awakes and begins its accustomed chores.

When the sun falls, when shadows vanish, and darkness covers the sky; when stray cats fight in alleys, wailing like babies, when streets lie empty, and prostitutes haggle with clients; when stars are covered by clouds, when gargoyles seem almost believable, and little motorized sweepers clean away the day-long droppings of dogs, on which many have stepped and received the benediction, *"Porte bonheur"* — this city becomes another, where shattered, lost lives emerge.

Its inhabitants are phalanxes of prostitutes, the males indistinguishable from the females, drug-pushers, who speak the politest French possible, furtive johns in cars whose motors seem to be more muffled than during the day, and hoards of winos, who can expertly play cards on the darkest of nights.

Both the pushers and the prostitutes are earnestly working, while the winos seem only to be killing time.

But all are surviving, busy converting the hours of the night into acquisition of some sort — *du fric*, the prostitute's fee, or an alcohol haze — just like the daytime inhabitants of this city, ever busy with their wages.

At night a fog descends upon Rouen, as if to give further cover to the secret desires that have slept during the day: the desire to get drunk, to do drugs, to have sex in dark alleys, to rob, to break, and at times, murder.

Perhaps when nothing comes of all that we want to do, and money, work, love become insubstantial as mist, perhaps it is then good to be awake at night; and perhaps there is joy in having torn pockets, a threadbare coat, worshipping twisted ideals. Perhaps daytime is for civilization and night for primordial needs and deeds.

Some friends and I had been drinking for most of the night, and instead of heading straight home, I felt like walking in the cold night to clear my head.

I walked 'til I came to the Cathedral, and there I sat down on the long cement blocks that serve as benches. The city was silent around me, and the moon stood fiercely bright, though the night was nearly spent.

Two benches away from me, hunched and huddled against the cold, sat a man whose teeth chattered loudly, and who burst into song now and then, his voice clear and strong. It went something like:

Skulldoor down, down crowfoot ground
shingled laughter, hoarfrost mound

I didn't really catch the rest, but it sounded like: wombdoor down, down underground sporic rhythm and spoor of sound. His tongue, thickened with drink and the cold, slurred and stuttered the rhyme. Where could he have picked up these words? Doggerel incantation?

I didn't ask him. But for some reason I did not leave and walk away either, despite a strong, sour odour of stale urine that exuded from him.

The strength of his voice jarred with his rather helpless posture. After a stifled belch, he sang again:

When I was young my mother sang to me
The gentlest songs of sleep;
And in the night she lit a fire bright:
My bed was warm and deep.

When I was a youth in life's full vigor
Sweetest joys I did reap.
And I did love a most beautiful girl
Whose heart was warm and deep.

"Ah! Jacques! Do you like my little song?"

I looked around expecting one of his cronies to respond. But there was only silence.

Then quickly he got up and came and sat beside me, clutching his arms to his chest. His rancid odour intensified.

"Ah! Jacques! Jacquot! Do I sing well?"

I told him that his was a good song for the cold.

He laughed in little spurts.

"You know, Jacques, I cannot remember my mother's face tonight. Can you help me, Jacquot? Describe her to me. You saw her often."

I said nothing, and gestured with my hands that I didn't know.

"My father's face I don't remember either. But then I don't remember my father. Did you bring any cider for us, Jacques?"

I said that I forgot all about it.

"Oh, it doesn't matter. Nothing serious."

Then he lunged away from me to the other side of the bench and vomited. His gags and belches were sharp and quick. He groaned for some time.

I should have left right away, but something, some fascination perhaps, held me there still. When he finished his groaning, he got up, hunched again, and carefully wiped his mouth.

"Christine will come soon. You'll like watching Christine. I do. We all do. Come, come with me!"

He rose from the bench and grabbed my arm to haul me away.

Perhaps I should have resisted, but I didn't.

We walked over to rue de Carmes.

"There's Robert sleeping. He says cider upsets his stomach."

Then standing over Robert, he straightened himself and pontificated loudly in derision:

"Next time we'll only give you the finest *eaux de vie,* your royal highness, your great majesty!"

Robert didn't stir. He lay in a dark pool of vomit that looked like blood.

We walked on, turning left on to rue aux Juifs, and then right on to rue du Bec, just behind the Palais de Justice.

It was very dark here, and each recess was the hiding place of a prostitute, all of whom ignored my guide, but made sure to greet me with a languid "Bonsoir."

"Where is she? Where? Where?" He was muttering to himself.

Then he stopped before a group of women struggling with a man; there were about six of them.

They swarmed the man; toppled him onto his back. Then stood over him.

"What do you think I am? A rabbit? A chicken for your stew pot? You owe me two hundred more."

The man on the ground tried to get up, but the women held him down, outraged, hurling profanities.

He tried to fight back, but one of the girls kicked him hard in the groin.

"Doesn't that feel better than before? Now pay her!"

The man groaned loudly.

They had stuffed his mouth with something.

"Search his pockets, girls!" It was the *fille* he had shortchanged. "He's not going home to his *nana*, all holy and innocent. Wait 'til she sees his empty pockets!"

She then turned to another girl who was approaching, and said:

"Imagine! He gives me a rolled up note. And when I unroll it, all it is, is a fifty! He thought he could be smart and cheap! *Salaud!*"

"Come on, Brigitte, we have his money. Here, here."

One of the girls got up and handed Brigitte all that was found in the man's pockets.

"Wait! Hold him!" Brigitte said coldly.

Slowly, she pulled up her short dress, and undulating her hips sensuously squatted over the man's face.

"Do you like what you see? Do you want more? Do you want to kiss it?"

There was a hissing noise, and the group howled and squeaked in delight.

Brigitte was getting her revenge.

She was pissing all over the man's face. He writhed and groaned, but the arms holding him down were tough and unrelenting.

Brigitte pissed slowly, in no hurry, as if what she did was an art that required singular care and absorption. Little wisps of steam rose between her thighs.

Then, as before, she twisted and swayed her bottom, as if she were enticing a lover to take her, and got up from the man's face, a rapturous smile on her face.

"Let the *salaud* go back to his *salope*."

She tugged a bit at her dress and said, "Ah, *putain! Flute! Ah, merde!* I lost the button to my dress! Annie, let me borrow your belt for tonight."

Annie wiggled her bottom quickly, pulled off a thin silver belt, and handed it over.

The drenched man slowly rolled over; the women spat on him and left in pairs, but not before delivering well-placed kicks.

"You're lucky we didn't slit your throat, you pig!" said the last girl, as she kicked him in the stomach, and walked away with an exaggerated feminine wriggle.

"Come on, Jacquot, come on! We don't want to be late! Come on, Christine is waiting!"

My guide pulled my coat-sleeve and half dragged me after him. I could hear his harsh panting breaths.

He ran in a hobbling gait, occasionally turning around to me, beckoning me with both his hands.

I followed him up rue Socrates all the way to where it turns into rue de l'Ecureuil, past rue Thiers and onto rue Villon. Here he stopped.

We were behind the Musée des Beaux-Arts.

My guide leaned against the pale wall of the building and vomited again, weakly, and then pulled me towards Square Verdrel.

In the dark trees of the park many little red glows appeared briefly as silent, waiting women brought cigarettes up to their lips.

My guide took me behind a garbage can and leaned heavily into me, forcing me down into an uncomfortable crouch.

"Look! Look! There she is! There's Christine!" His voice was an excited, high-pitched whisper.

I looked to where he was pointing.

Beneath a tree, barely lit by a street lamp on rue Jeanne-d'Arc, stood a tall, young woman in a very large and bulky fur coat. A middle-aged man had his arms around her, while she was loosening his pants, which soon dropped to his ankles.

She swung back her coat; underneath she was naked.

With an almost graceful gesture, she slid her arms above her until she embraced the tree.

The man plunged into her fiercely; she responded by gripping him tight with her legs.

My guide squealed with delight, covering his mouth with both hands.

Then he fumbled around in his oversized coat, and from deep inside it he took out — a dead cat.

He held the animal's face out towards Christine and her *passe*.

The cat was very stiff. Its lips were pulled back tightly, revealing its bluish teeth, between which its blackened tongue stuck out, as though in ridicule. Its opened eyes were frosted white and glinted in the dim light of the park; its tail was half torn off and hung behind like a limp shoelace.

With great vigor my guide began to move the cat back and forth, trying to imitate Christine's hurried, spasmodic jerks.

"See, Jacques! See, Jacquot!"

But this time he wasn't talking to me. He was talking to the cat. He seemed to have forgotten that I was there.

As Christine hurried to finish off her *passe*, the cat moved faster as well.

With great finesse my guide moved the dead animal's pelvis in quick, short thrusts. The cat now was in perfect harmony with Christine's speed and rhythm.

Perhaps because of my guide's clutching hands, or because of the rapid movement, a horrible rotting smell started to come from the cat, just as the *passe* lunged hard into Christine for the last time, and gave voice to a deep grunt.

My stomach churned.

I pushed away from that garbage can and my self-appointed guide, who obviously wanted to spend the whole night watching Christine earn her *fric.*

As my gorge heaved, I began to run — away from that park, away from Christine, and most of all away from my guide, from his strong-voiced songs, his stale urine smell, and that rotting cat, held tight, passionately, lovingly.

I ran into Allée Eugène-Delacroix where rats scattered from my feet, and then cut across onto rue Saint-Lô, which I followed west until I hit rue Jeanne-d'Arc once again. I continued running all the way down to the Seine.

In front of the Place des Arts, my stomach began to feel calmer; I stopped and drew breath.

I slouched down beneath Corneille's huge statue, looking with him out to the resting river, whose waters now seemed as black as the dead cat's tongue.

I sat there unmoving. Perhaps hours passed, perhaps only a few minutes.

And as I stood leaning on Corneille, who pensively held his quill over a sheaf of paper, I saw the dawn creeping up, to my left, gilding the dark clouds.

I was stiff and frozen; my nose leaked, and I could barely feel my fingers or my feet; yet I stood there and with tired eyes and a dizzy head greeted the sun's rebirth.

I watched 'til the first light struck the waters of the Seine like a gesture of grace.

Come clear dawn, tear the hem of the sky wherein treasures hide unseen. Change the bones of the sleeping dead so that they may dance in the joy of your coming. With my ears I listen, with my hands I await. Lift the feet of mountains into nimble step. Make the waters and the dews to flow in expectation; let them not hold back the joy of their becoming. The hush behind the wind is your secret language as the slow curl of fire remembers high-shooting flames that have licked away countless cities, unending faces. Teach me your dance; breathe on my muted lips so that they may prophesy. Kiss my hands into freedom and bring my body to completion . . .

CHAPTER 8

FOR A VILLAGE TO HAVE ITS OWN HOLY MAN was deemed a privilege, and every day women came to the walnut tree, some even from neighbouring villages, with the customary offerings — mostly food they had prepared.

Bawa-ji kept nothing for himself but gave it all to the children, who would stop by their erstwhile school, before running home to the village.

For long hours, Bawa-ji would assume some yogic posture and not move. He undertook fasts that lasted a week or more. Because of these spiritual obligations, we conversed less and less.

Raj continued teaching the children in the apricot grove, just beside the first wheatfield, where the Piplan Nadi made a little detour before rushing off to converge with the mighty Beas River, far to the South.

One day, Raj took me along as a "guest" before whom his students could recite.

There were about twenty boys and girls, aged five to fourteen, all eager-faced, coyly smiling. They looked at Raj, who gave them the signal, and they burst into a raucous:

Sur le pont d'Avignon
On y dance, on y dance.
Sur le pont d'Avignon

On y dance tous en rond.
Les belles dames font comme ça,
Et puis encore comme ça . . .

The older ones looked embarrassed, while the youngsters sang in a full-throated abandon, bouncing their knees to the rhythm.

I applauded loudly.

The students giggled; some of the older boys kicked at the grass. The younger ones seemed ready to do it all over again.

Raj was teaching these children, as he would have taught his own — not by giving them boundaries. Their enthusiasm moved me. Most, if not all of them, would never have any use for French after they grew up — but now, as children, it was a language steeped in magic, speaking of far away lands.

Their happiness was contagious, and I volunteered to buy them all ice-cream after school; we agreed to meet at the general store. And with that I let them get on with their lessons. I think mathematics was next.

I made my way back to the house and began to copy another journal entry.

Why was I going through this exercise? I did not rightly know. But what I read held a fascination: there was something here that spoke deeply to me.

Looking up from my makeshift desk, I saw Bawa-ji to the right under his walnut tree, and down a little, to the left, was the apricot grove academy. East and West. The twain do, and must, meet. Raj seemed at home in both. I could not call him an oxymoron for he was happy in both worlds. A man must resolve his contradictions if he can, just as he must strive to be both happy and useful. And in Dhanoa, Raj was both.

Journal Entry: Madame Arlette

In this wide and rich earth, there are many things we can possess and so many that forever elude our grasp. Perhaps this is the balance of true freedom — but in the labyrinth that Rouen was for me in those first years, this realization was denied me, for I circled like a bird of prey that keeps looking for movement in a barren land, never returning to the place where it last perched. In the twists and turns of streets, alleyways, and roads, I was seeking an ever-shifting centre, an Ithaca for my heart.

My life unwound from a very slow spool. I moved from one rented flat to another, as though I were a pilgrim who stays briefly for a night to rest his head before going off in search of another more distant roof beneath which to dream of splendour or redemption.

It was at that very old, cross-timbered house on rue des Fossés Louis-VIII that I first entered the liquid maze of dreams.

A peculiar house it was, but I was drawn to it, and ended up renting a room there for nearly four months. The woodwork of that house was said to date from the time of William the Conqueror, or so the landlady, Madame Arlette, told me; and the many rafters and beams in the ceiling of the main room were ebony-black and shiny with the wear of many lives. A musty odour, not entirely unpleasant, pervaded the entire house. And if a ray of the sun occasionally made its way through a thick-paned window, it was quickly reduced to a watery reflection, swarming with dust motes.

Madame Arlette, whose family name I never got to know, was a large, morose, red-faced woman of about forty-five. She always wore a very long dark green apron, and loosely tied her thin, pale hair with either a red or a blue hairband. One of her peculiar habits was to stare past you, if you asked her any sort of question at all. She would stand awkwardly and, after a lengthy space of silence, cast her eyes down and mumble a brief reply. It impressed me that she could boil an answer down to a few words, no matter how convoluted the question. But if she spoke on her own initiative, she would utter at least a few sentences, and even sometimes smile.

I was the only lodger at her house though there was room for four or five more people, and the rent was reasonable. I lived in the top-most room. From the window, I had a good view of the street below, as well as the spires of the high Cathedral, named Notre Dame, like all the cathedrals in France.

When Madame Arlette had shown me the entire house, room-by-room, she led me upstairs, and handed me two keys, one for the front door and the other to my room. Then she stood there, as if waiting for me to say something. So I thanked her, praised the layout of the house and said that I would be right back with my things that I had left at a friend's place.

I worked in a bakery in those days, and I kept ungodly hours. I had to be at work by 3:30 A.M., when we would scrape out the high mounds of dough, knead them in the dough press, and then cut off small rounds for baguettes, and double that for regular-sized loaves. These rounds we threw onto a long, floured table where Monsieur Jobin, the master *boulanger*, pressed and kneaded each piece with his knuckles and then quickly shaped it into a baguette, using the entire length of his forearm. By 7:30, four hundred loaves were baked crisp and golden, and all of us, working around the huge ovens, looked like worn-out wraiths, covered as we were with flour.

I worked seven days a week, on the same schedule, with two days off every three weeks.

I was soon back at the house with my things and found Madame Arlette still waiting beside my room's door, where I had left her some fifteen minutes before.

I smiled and began to fit the key to the latch, all the while carrying on some trite monologue about the fineness of the summer's day outside. She just stood there with her hands in her apron pockets, and then, as I opened my door:

"You don't need to worry about anything here."

I took this to mean that the house was solid and the plumbing fine, and I said something to this effect.

"You don't need to worry about anything here," she repeated.

And then added as an after-thought:

"There *is* a cat buried beside the doorstep. Don't worry. I saw it myself. I dug it up the day my uncle died and reburied it after his funeral."

I nodded firmly, as though reassured that the supernatural fence, once so essential for all Norman houses and public buildings, was indeed in place.

She took something from her apron and held it up before me. It was the shriveled forepaw of a cat; the retracted skin revealed tiny claws, black as the ancient timbers of the house.

With this emphatic conclusion, she left, and I was allowed to enter my new quarters.

The room was small, yet not so small that it was uncomfortable. The bathroom and toilet were down the hall, and I could cook my meals downstairs in the kitchen, where Madame Arlette spent most of her time. The kitchen was her hearth, warm and living, the only place where she ever seemed content.

As I arranged my few things, the room began to take on my identity and became familiar. Below the window, I placed my books, and on the windowsill went my two ivory Netsukes, picked up at the antique market for a few francs.

But my first night at that house was difficult.

Since I had to get up so early, I went to bed before ten. But just as I felt the first pull of sleep, I heard Madame Arlette going noisily up and down the stairs. I had noted earlier that she moved about the house noiselessly as a cat, but now each footfall was a loud thump, as if she weighed a ton. I can't recall how many times she went up and down the stairs, but each time it was faster and louder.

Then, I heard her croon softly by my door; it was something about the moonlight and the nightingale singing happily from tree to tree the whole night long. I sighed and hoped to God that Madame Arlette would not follow the example of the joyous nightingale.

As her song subsided, and she must have repeated each verse at least four times, I heard something drop; it sounded heavy, almost like a barrel; and I followed each thud, step after step, until the object landed with a squashed thump near the front door.

And, while she was having a loud conversation with herself in the kitchen, at last the weight of fatigue drew me under, and I sank into a soft dream.

~~~

I am on a knoll with high grass
and the sun is hidden,
but not behind clouds.
It is lost to the sky.
A voice echoes
but I cannot answer though I want to.
It is the voice of a woman calling;
and as she calls
the grass grows higher around me;
but I cannot answer,
for I am not grass;
and waters rise around me as she calls again;
but I cannot answer,
for I am not water.
A third time she calls
and mountains raise their heads;
but I cannot answer,
for I am not earth or stone.
I would swim
but I know there is no shore.
I would fly but I know there is no sky.
I would run but I know there is no land.
Only water and this green knoll.
Who are you? I ask.
She does not answer.
On my lips
she places the disk of the moon
and my soul bursts
like the flare that is the Milky Way.
She touches my forehead
with the clear light of the sun
and my heart becomes a blue lotus
tossed upon the flow of creation.

She lets me rise.
She embraces me.
She speaks her name.
Helena. Helena. Helena.
How blessed is the gift of your presence.
Wherever I turn you are there,
hidden behind the face of clouds,
dancing among motes in a sunbeam.
Helena. Helena. Helena.
Thrice-blessed.
She kisses my right shoulder . . .

A scream struck me down like a swath of grass before a sickle.

~~~

I jumped out of bed. It was Madame Arlette running around downstairs screeching like a banshee. I tugged on some pants and a shirt and raced out of my room.

I caught up with her in the kitchen, her hair loose, her apron-strings untied. Wordlessly she screamed, the veins of her neck popping, her face a bluish red. Then she had a violent coughing fit.

I held her arms and asked her to calm down. She tore herself away and stood by the stove, trying with shaking hands to tie her apron.

It was 2:30 in the morning. Time anyway for me to get ready and go to work.

She said nothing but merely turned and walked away. I heard her go to her room by the foot of the stairs and gently shut the door.

I went upstairs, washed, dressed and came back to the kitchen to make myself some coffee. I could see nothing unusual in the house that might have caused those screams, which had tore me from my dream. Perhaps she, poor woman, had been visited by a nightmare.

It was time to leave. I put everything out of my head and went out into the street. It was very dark out, but here and there I passed people for whom the previous day was just ending, on their way home to bed. I eyed them with some envy.

All of us at the bakery tended the needs of yeast, flour and water, the magical trinity that transubstantiated simple elements into the blessed body that is the staff of life. Monsieur Jobin never tired of telling us that bread was the perfection of civilization. And in that, he would point out, as we toiled and sweated over the rising dough, it was part of a larger trinity. There was bread, there was wine, and there was cheese — upon these three, human civilization itself was founded. These three foods could not be found in themselves in nature; rather they needed the hand of man to build them, construct them, just as cities and ocean-going ships and airplanes did.

As we slit the top of the oven-ready loaves with razor blades, Monsieur Jobin, his own duties done, would lecture us. The wild yeast is harnessed and its transmuting force tamed and trained to push foods, lowly in their natural states, to take on a higher, more sublime flavour, texture and taste. In our flour-encrusted workplace, Monsieur Jobin's pronouncements rose like his breads into great and worthy homilies.

We had finished the day's baking and were relaxing for a spell before starting the batch for the next day. Monsieur Jobin observed that I looked tired, and then gave me a light hearted warning about staying up late with friends and drinking. I laughed and told him the antics of Madame Arlette.

His eyes widened: "Who did you say?"

"Madame Arlette. I rent a room from her."

"What?! But why, my friend? No one in Rouen would live with her. She is very strange in the head, you know. You've have me worried." I could tell he was not joking with me.

But before he could expand on the hazards that I was facing at Madame Arlette's, the demands of the dough summoned us. Soon we were busy measuring out the flour, mixing in the salt, pitching the yeast, and adding warm water and sourdough. What we left behind were three huge white mounds that would swell and grow in the dark, moist warmth all day long.

After my shift, I walked back to my flat and, as I entered, Madame Arlette met me at the front door. There was a loud honking and hissing coming from the kitchen.

"I've just bought a goose," she informed me.

Then something very big and white half-flew, half-waddled past me and went up the stairs.

"*La vache!* I didn't tie it up properly," Madame Arlette whispered fiercely, as she chased after the bird. More amused than anything, I followed close behind.

The goose had got in the bathroom and into the tub where its webbed feet helped not at all. It slipped around, honking loudly; and when it saw us it hissed savagely, its pale tongue stuck out, pink and rigid.

Quickly Madame threw a towel over it, and then picked it up, holding the towel tight over the bird's head. Perhaps sensing the inevitable, the goose stopped struggling and resorted to an occasional hiss.

I left them there, but a few minutes later Madame Arlette called up the stairs. "Monsieur, can you please come and help me?" I went down to the kitchen to see what she wanted.

The goose was still in her hands, but the towel was gone. And the once graceful neck of the bird now ended in a bloody stump, which Madame held over a deep yolk-yellow bowl. She motioned to me, and thrust the goose in my hands.

I held the carcass by the feet and pointed its neck into the bowl. A thin stream of blood was squirting in dark little gushes — the last few pumps of the heart. The goose quivered slightly as I slid my hand down from its feet to hold it by its wing. A heavy sweat drenched the skin beneath the feathers. After a while, the squirts gave way to large, round drops of blood that fell like dark pearls into the yellow bowl.

"Drain it well, if you please," Madame Arlette instructed, "I can make some excellent black sausage with the blood. And I'll use a little of it tonight to thicken the soup."

She left the kitchen and returned holding a large straw basket.

"The down I'll use to make a nice pillow."

She took the still warm bird from me, and sat down on one of the kitchen chairs. Soon she was busy, expertly plucking the feathers. The living creature had quickly become a thing of utility.

I returned upstairs and went straight to my bath to wash away the flour and the smell of blood. Water is the greatest of gifts, and as I lay there my dream was restored.

Helena. Who was she? What was she? How did my mind come up with her?

How singular was her beauty, how luminous her eyes. What colour were they? I could not recall. There was a brightness encircling her as there is around a cluster of roses, bowed.

When I went downstairs to make dinner, the kitchen bore no sign either of the slaughtered goose, or Madame Arlette. I had some dry sausage, with bread and cheese, and some cherries that had just appeared in the market, and went off to bed.

But I did not dream of Helena again for a very long time.

I stayed for more than three months at Madame Arlette's; and all those days were filled with surprises, even as my hours at work were a pile of drudgery and fatigue.

It was August now and summer began to yield to flashing rain. An early chill in the air spoke of the autumn ahead — both the harvest and a certain lazy abandonment of the land before the storms and torrents of winter.

My summer's harvest consisted of countless baguettes and Madame Arlette's oddities.

How often I helped her singe the hairs off a pig's head, or scrape the scales from a perch or bream.

She shaved a sow's head, once, with my razor.

How often she would see people that weren't there.

Sometimes she would leave a glass of wine and some bread on the kitchen table for these unseen "guests." And when I would go into the kitchen early in the morning to make coffee, before work, the bread would be gone and the wine glass empty.

Of course, I was sure, Madame herself ate and drank what was there, just to prove to me that the other-worldly was as close as one wished it to be — all one had to do was to hold out one's hand and someone, something would indeed take hold.

How many times I heard her scream incomprehensibly in the night. How many times she ran up and down the stairs.

Once I saw her cut her palm in the kitchen, as she sliced through a potato — she did not know I was behind her — and she muttered a blood-charm: *"Sinew to sinew, bone to bone, blood to blood as if they were glued,"* and the bleeding at once stopped. That skill, at least, I would like to have learned from her.

Whenever she stepped outside the house, with her large canvas bag for groceries, she seemed cheerful and vivacious. She would make sure to greet everyone and had a polite word for all the shopkeepers. She looked like any other middle-aged, middle-class housewife shopping for her family's lunch or dinner. But the minute she entered the house, she changed, and became the morose, awkward, sullen Madame Arlette that I knew.

One night just as I had gone to bed, she burst into my room. This she had never done before. I just stared at her.

Speaking gravely, as though with great dread, she said, "Tonight is a heavy night. I must watch. If I close my eyes just once, we are lost."

And then she added, "Tomorrow, the banks and the post office will be closed. Are you prepared?"

Having dispensed her dire warning, she stood quietly for a long moment, almost apologetically, with her head down, as though in a contrite pose.

I thanked her for her kindness and managed a smile.

Still silent, she walked backwards, wished me a good night, and then softly closed the door, as if not to disturb me. I didn't even hear her go back down the stairs.

When I came home that evening, after working a double-shift, she was in my room, waiting in the dark.

I jumped back startled when I turned the light on and saw her on my chair. Her eyes had that distant look, staring past me, her lank hair hanging free. Without a word, she got up and walked out, closing the door behind her.

Almost immediately she knocked softly, and when I opened she said, "You should not drink tap water. Remember, bottled water only." With that, she went down the stairs.

I did not hold it against her. She was an eccentric — and I needed the room. An odd balance, but a balance nonetheless.

The next day I did put in a hook-and-eye lock on my door; it was the best I could manage short of launching into a serious installation project. I thought it would suffice.

However, the next week was my last at Madame Arlette's house. In fact, so much happened that week that I still have difficulty in piecing everything together.

Late into the night I would hear her moaning as if someone were slowly and cruelly torturing her. Objects flying about had become a common occurrence for me. Some nights I could hear the sound of large wings in my room.

One time, Madame Arlette tossed me an apple as I stood by the stove making supper; she had bought some at the market. The apple vanished in mid-air before it reached me. I couldn't find it anywhere, though I looked in every conceivable place, behind the cupboard, underneath the chairs, I even moved the refrigerator, but to no avail. All the while Madame Arlette smiled at my growing confusion.

That night, as I went up after dinner, I thought I saw someone crouched against the wall at the top of the stairs.

A crumpled figure of a man wearing a long, extremely wrinkled great coat of a dirty, dark colour. His face seemed streaked with soot. He held his hands close to his chest, and his eyes were blank, white ovals, with no pupils. Yet, I knew he could see everything. I felt the hair at the back of my neck rise in fear.

I could not hear Madame Arlette anywhere.

The house was perfectly still.

I had to go past him to get to my room, and he was not disappearing, as figments are wont to do. Rather, he crouched against the wall, as though waiting for me to make a move, when he would pounce. I stood still.

Then, I slowly turned around, went down the stairs, grabbed a large rolling pin from the kitchen, and again came up the stairs. He was gone. But there was an odd smell in the landing, a caustic, soapy smell.

I kept the rolling pin beside me on the bed, and locked my door with the flimsy hook.

That night I had my second dream of Helena; and she appeared more beautiful than before . . .

~~~

I am in a watered land.
I am holding up my hands to the sun in the east.
Hail, my lady,
the grain glistens in the furrow.
How alluring are the poppies in ripening fields.
As I summon her, Helena appears,
wearing a crown of lapis lazuli and gold.
The robe she wears contains all the wonders of the earth
flowers of every hue,
the flash of broad-backed rivers,

the swell of fruits,
the brightness of air.
And her words are gentle as the new moon.
"What I say to you,
let singers weave into song.
The bowl of heaven lies empty, unused.
What will fill it?"
And from me rises a tree,
a high cedar;
and from the ground grasses grow high.
A weight holds me down,
and I speak to her from below.
Helena, your breasts are a golden field
which pour out breath, and grain,
and many well-watered meadows.
Touch again my lips into song.
And her hands,
which are as fair as the North Star,
as soft as the breeze of spring
moving through a sprouting garden,
these she places on my chest.
She kneels beside me.
she takes my head onto her lap.
I look at her face,
more beautiful than the waking dawn,
at her eyes that are the colour of emeralds,
held against the light.
With her hands she molds me
and I become a garden carefully tended.
And now Helena strides a lion.
An aureate splendour rises from her,
like two wings.
She holds fire in her right hand
and water in her left.

With her eyes she beckons me to stand beside her.
She speaks:
"Who rises in the night
and pours out his heart like water?
My breathing has no ear,
and if I put my mouth in the dust
will I know the shape of hope?"
Her lion stands quiet in its tawny strength.
Pour out, my lady, I say to her
and I shall drink all that you offer.
And Helena offers me a rose, blue as the Nile.
Her feet are soon caught
in the flow of a dance
and with her hands shaping speech,
she goes to the horizon
like the setting sun.
I cannot follow,
for my feet are bound to stones . . .

~~~

A round shape. A round, smooth, shape. A round, smooth, cool shape. A shape nice to hold, fitting perfectly in my hand.

I am holding something.

This realization instantly awakens me.

I sit up.

And in my hand?

I grope for the light.

Something heavy falls from the bed.

The light.

And I see.

I have an apple in my hand; and I must have fallen asleep clutching the rolling pin; that is what fell to the floor as I reached for the light. But I could not remember bringing an apple to my room. I never eat in bed.

My head was too fogged to explain. I put the apple beside the clock. It was 2:30 again — no point in trying to sleep now. Before I opened the door, I checked my little lock. It was still latched.

On my way to the bakery, I thought about Helena. I never had had a recurring dream before. She was all beauty and all peace. Beyond that I did not know. I could stand close beside her, but not possess her; and she went where I could not follow. Perhaps I was not meant to understand; just experience. An inexplicable sadness lingered with me the whole of that day.

When I came home, Madame Arlette was not there. I made my dinner, ate it, took a bath, and ironed a few shirts in my room.

I heard something roll down the stairs.

When I went to check, I found an apple lying there in the hall. It was warm in my hand as I took it to the kitchen and put it in the fruit basket. Among the oranges, it was the only apple, dark red. I was not going to eat that, no matter what.

I returned to my room.

Soon after, I heard Madame Arlette come in and go straight to her room. I finished my ironing and took a newspaper into bed.

There was a quietness in the house, a stillness that I hadn't sensed before. It was as if a great noise had suddenly ended.

My eyes scanned an article about the Grand Prix circus, the Rouen-les-Essarts, where Alberto Ascari set one of the fastest time en route, in 1952, in his Ferrari. He was followed by the likes of Fangio, Gurney, Brabham, Ickx,

Surtees, and Jo Schlesser, who burned to death in a fiery crash.

But I could not concentrate. I definitely needed to move out.

Tomorrow was my day off, so I promised myself that this would be my last night at Madame Arlette's house. Any place would be saner that this.

I also noticed that the apple I had placed near my bed was gone.

Since that time, it has become my personal philosophy to avoid even thinking about the supernatural in order not to attract things I cannot control.

But that night, I dreamt of Helena for the last time.

~~~

In the first of days,
In the first of nights,
In the first of years,
I float towards a shore.
And suddenly I am with Helena,
in her garden.
Her robe is woven from spring flowers:
every colour in nature
with the gold of her skin shining through.
Her fingers wash over
my forehead, eyes, face, lips
like streams of lustral water.
Her breasts hold the span of my breath,
and my shallow knowledge fails
on the skin of her belly.
Her hair is the net
that binds me to her.
She breathes upon me,
holding my face in her hands.

I feel her heart beat against me.
Her hands tell me that I must fall
and she will hold me.
The trace of rivers is her rushing blood;
her beading skin foretells my tears of tomorrow.
Her eyes close so gently,
and I break in her softness.
The rhythm
of her breathing holds me,
and laying my head on her breast
I sleep . . .

~~~

It was mid-morning when I awoke. My room was filled with sunlight — rare this late in the season. And it was wonderful to watch the day grow and not have to rush off to work.

A flurry of wings; quarrelsome chirping came from outside my window. I got up and parted the curtains.

Just on the ledge, some house sparrows were fighting over something. But they saw the curtain move and darted away.

I opened the window to see what had caused the commotion.

There was nothing there.

But as I was closing the window, something caught the sunlight and shimmered.

In a crack of the windowsill was a hair, long and golden blonde.

I picked it up and measured its length with my fingers.

Had she left me a sign?

Joy washed over me.

And I put the hair, for safekeeping, in my trusty journal.

149

Madame had been silent all night, for once, and the house was still quiet.

Great, I thought. Just when I decide to move, she decides to become normal.

I was to spend that day looking at flats I'd chosen from various advertisements and friends' recommendations.

Monsieur Jobin was coming over in a little while to help me in my search. He had promised to make sure I got a decent place.

But none of this happened, because my first sight of Madame Arlette that morning changed everything.

There she was in the hallway, hanging from the black central beam.

She'd used a pale stocking, stretched tight and thin for a noose. Her eyes bulged red, and she had bitten through her tongue, which stuck out, an obscene blue specked with dried spit and blood. Her head rested stiffly on her right shoulder.

She was neatly dressed, with hair perfectly in place, tied back with a blue hairband. A high stool lay toppled beneath her; and on the dark grey flagstone floor, there was a squashed apple, perhaps mashed by her foot before she climbed up the stool; its pulp was rusted brown.

I stood frozen on the stairs.

Just then someone knocked on the door, loudly and long.

I stumbled to the door, past the rigid corpse.

It was Monsieur Jobin.

He stared, as I had, at Madame Arlette in mid-air.

He shook his head slowly. "Poor, poor woman."

I went through to the lounge and phoned the police. "Touch nothing," they told me.

Monsieur Jobin and I sat in the lounge, waiting wordlessly.

Soon, there was a hard knock at the door, and three gendarmes let themselves in.

They, too, stared quietly at Madame Arlette, hanging perfectly still, until some ambulance attendants pushed past them and began to let down the body.

They lowered her gently to the ground, and as they laid her on the cold flagstones, something fell from her apron.

One gendarme picked it up.

It was the cat's paw she'd shown me when I first moved in.

He carefully put it into a plastic bag.

The attendants loosened the stocking and bore Madame Arlette to the stretcher, covering her with a white sheet and tying her down. In this way, they carried her out the door, where a crowd had gathered.

The gendarmes rummaged around in her room, and eventually found something in a little straw basket filled with goose feathers.

Her suicide note.

At the police station, I was briefly shown the note written in a childish hand. The task of continually watching and guarding against the dark forces was too much, it said; she could not bear to live any longer.

Madame Arlette lay in the morgue for three weeks. Nobody came to claim her body. Not even the authorities knew her family name, or anything else about her. She was nameless and faceless already in death's great bureaucracy.

In a simple coffin of grey wood, and on a cold October day, beneath hovering clouds and a raw wind, we buried Madame Arlette. Monsieur Jobin, some of the staff from the bakery, and I were the only mourners.

The old house reverted to the city and stayed empty for some years. Eventually it was sold off to someone from Paris.

Years passed. I moved on to other things, another life, and Monsieur Jobin sold his bakery and moved down south to Marseilles. I still get the occasional phone call from him; every time he invites me to come visit, an invitation I have yet to take up.

But every October 9th, I go to the cemetery and place some flowers on Madame Arlette's grave.

Each time it is harder to find the little stone plaque with her name and date of death. I clear the weeds and the grass that grow over her, but time is their ally.

How quickly monuments to the dead decay. I am no Catholic, yet I find myself in the Cathedral, now and then, lighting a candle for the repose of that tormented soul.

And I still have that long, golden hair which I found on that fateful morning. It rests in my journal, where I first placed it.

Sometimes, when I am writing, I turn back the pages to that hair. And it still glistens, as my fingers gently stroke it. It is no longer important to whom it belongs — a plaything of the wind, no doubt. It's an emblem for me of my search for love.

Poor Madame Arlette sought this love in the unseen, but found only dark forces. I hope she found peace at last.

An immense distance sometimes lies between the world we inhabit in our dreams and the waking world. Can we connect them through the companionship of death?

I replace the hair in its hiding place, close the journal, and return it to the shelf.

The hour ends the day.

In the Book of Love are many names; some are hidden, say the mystics, some revealed . . .

CHAPTER 9

UNLIKE RAJ, I HAD GROWN UP IN CANADA, in various small southern Ontario towns; my childhood was filled with hayrides, camping, long drives in the country, and when I was older, hunting trips to the bush.

I had come to India with the usual expectations: timely revelations, meaningful discoveries, intimate connections with a mysterious old country. I had meant to undertake a sentimental journey through a land constructed from personal mythology and very little reality. It wasn't long before I realized that personal mythology mattered little in the turgid flow that is India, for it does not, perhaps cannot, separate mythology from history: Ravana is just as real as a sprawling chemical factory; and gods and demons infest the air like the pollution that leaves an oily ring around a shirt collar. Wherever I went, I found almost what I was looking for; but something was missing, eluding my grasp, slipping away, which would mirror the image of India I had constructed in my mind. All I found was ghostly grandeur, like a skeletal, crumbling, sinuous Mughal tomb whose gardens have long been swallowed by ramshackle shanties.

Perhaps the India I sought for existed only in my imagination. It was the fourteenth-century Arab traveller, Ibn Battuta, who described Indian culture as — a few pearls in a lot of gravel.

One evening, Bawa-ji asked me what would make me really happy?

I could not answer him.

"My friend, Dhanoa is not your world. Curiosity only has made you stay here," he pointed to the walnut tree as he spoke. Was the place where he sat an illusion for him?

"And neither is Raj's world your own. I know you are reading his account of his time in France. He read me a passage from that journal two years ago, when I first visited Dhanao. He has found some peace, because he knows now that life can be a bundle of pain, which we must all carry on our backs, no matter what. It is our lot. We cannot run away from this burden. And it is in this sorrow that we must live, and work, and laugh. This is what I told Raj, once; and look at him now. Content even in Dhanoa, after growing up in *Vilayat*. My friend, you must know how to be happy even in an empty room.

"You must let opposites live within yourself, my young friend."

"What do you mean by opposites," I asked him.

"You see, you are not a Punjabi because you were raised far away in Canada, and yet you speak Punjabi, and even understand some Pashto." Here, Bawa-ji chuckled softly, perhaps remembering when he pulled me from the car wreck.

"You've come here looking for something that you'll never find. The Punjab is not your home; it will never be. You are only chasing the ghosts of your ancestors here; and perhaps these ghosts want to be left in peace."

Bawa-ji smiled, but he was no longer looking at me; his eyes were turned to the mountains — with yearning.

"One day, I too will go home." His words were barely a whisper.

I sat before him in all my blindness.

He took up his rosary and slowly counted a few beads. "Remember, my friend, fruit is valued not for its rind, but for its flesh."

Journal Entry: Philippe

The Eure is a slow, winding river that takes its path like a wanderer who has no real destination. As it meanders deep inside Normandy, it touches the very heart of this land, where history and love are inseparable as melody from song. It's a broad-backed river, and its waters are a deep green that flow with an even rhythm, like the sleep of a young woman, adrift in the current of dreams.

The Eure wanders out towards Les Andelys, where the Chateau Gaillard, Richard the Lionhearted's fort, tops a mountain crag; just a few crumbled walls now, but the view from high up is mesmeric. If you stand there long enough, looking down at the serpentine Eure, you can hear Blondel singing that fabled song as he wandered Europe looking for Richard his master who pined for two years in an Austrian dungeon, waiting to be ransomed. Each wanderer has his song; without a song, perhaps you can't be a wanderer: *"Ja nus hons pris ne dira sa raison; adroitement, se dolantement non . . . "*

It's been a long time since I've returned to this Chateau.

Yes, it was with Philippe. It was on a June day we climbed that hillside, and stood by the pale shale walls and looked down at the Eure. It was very still there, as only ruins can be still; we stood silent together in the dust of ages.

Yes, Philippe had his song; but he wandered too far without it. I still play the tape sometimes that he gave me, his renderings of works by Rameau, and I marvel still at the strength of his playing. Such a contrast — the power

156

he had over the harpsichord, the momentum and grace — with those almost skeletal hands, the fragility of his body, the dark, haunted eyes.

And I must also remember why he gave me that tape. It was gratitude — gratitude for the money I gave him that day at the Chateau to get his heroin fix. I watched him for a long time walk down the winding path.

Language fails, but music forever succeeds. Music is the labyrinth through which our frailties glimpse the eternal forms. Philippe was Rameau on that tape, and always will be.

Hushed Eure, run softly, 'til I end my song . . .

CHAPTER 10

RAJ'S OTHER LIFE, IN THAT FAR AWAY NORMAN CITY, became ever more real to me. I had never been to Rouen; nor to France, for that matter. My only connection to French culture was Montreal, where I was living, with frequent trips to Quebec City.

But this distant, abstracted, rainy French city became in my mind a place where opposites met and harmonized: the past with the future, the bitter with the sweet.

I asked Raj one day what made him begin his journal.

"I wrote," he told me, "so the dead could speak, and to remember those still living."

"Would they recognize me, though," his right hand explored his clipped beard, "here in Dhanoa, where I teach little French songs to Punjabi children?"

"Do you ever want to go back to Rouen?"

"Go back to what? There is no one waiting for me there. My memories are already many, many years old. Life has moved on, tossing me here along the way." He looked up at the mulberry tree, got to his feet, and carefully picked off a piece of dead bark.

"No, France holds only sadness for me. And if I went back, I would be even more of a stranger than I am here." He folded his arms across his chest, and leaned against the trunk.

Then he added in Punjabi:

"And besides, I am tired of being complicated. France is an unreal country for me now. I exist, and that is enough; I cannot go back to past happiness. Time cannot be recreated."

"But do you want to stay in Dhanoa forever? You have so many talents and abilities. Why waste them here?" Even as I spoke, I was struck by the stupidity of my comments. The words of Bawa-ji came back to me: Raj's world was not my own.

"Teaching little children anywhere is not a waste, is it?" he smiled with mockery. "And neither are my talents so very unique. The earth in her august abundance produces many men far greater than I am."

He walked back from the tree and sat beside me, though his arms lay folded across his chest still.

"Don't you see? I am at peace here. Dhanoa has been my salvation, my little place of sanity, my sanctuary. This remote village has given me happiness. It has taken away my pain. Long ago, when my world fell apart, I began to flee from my history and my own self. And when I stopped running, I was here, in Dhanoa. I know the villagers laugh at me behind my back. They are natives, and I am not; though I look like them. I know what they say: 'There goes that funny, odd man who lived in *Vilayat*; he must have been kicked out of there for something; why else would he come here and leave the paradise of *Vilayat*?' But despite all that, they do send their children to me. And I teach them to the best of my ability. This is what I am now. Yes, I am a *Kaatha-Sahib,* which is what the villagers call me; the English have translated this term rather well with their expression, WOG, Westernized Oriental Gentleman. That is exactly what I truly am."

He laughed to himself, and placed his elbows on his knees and leaned forward to examine a long line of ants that was slowly marching off with small bits of dry mulberry.

I had no answer or reply for him. Each one of us must construct his own truth.

The winter wheat was much higher around us now, so that it gave a deep soughing whenever the wind passed by; and the nightingales sang every evening still in the apricot grove, their song merging with the murmur of the Piplan Nadi, whose waters gleamed in the light of the pale winter moon . . .

Journal Entry: Ithaca

I was living on rue Bouquet, just beside the Gare at the edge of the run down red light district, when dream became reality for me.

I was having lunch at La Suisse, a bistro on rue de la République.

It was a good place to sit in if you had some time to kill, because there was always someone to talk to you.

My friend Marcel worked there. He was short and heavy set. "A good Norman peasant," he described himself.

In fact, I can even remember exactly what I had ordered for lunch, an *omelette aux herbes,* which wasn't especially Swiss, but then nothing on the menu was.

As I waited for my order, a group walked in, laughing, joking, talking loudly.

Among them was a girl — who, as the poet says, "walked in beauty . . . "

Her poise, her grace, the way her eyes took in the world around her — plunged me into another world altogether.

Someone gave me a rough push on the shoulder.

It was Marcel.

He had put down the omelet in front of me.

"Wake up! It's time to eat!"

Then he turned to see what I was staring at.

He whistled softly through his teeth.

"Oh-la-la-la-la!"

"Exactly."

"Who is she?" he asked. Now we were both staring.

"I was going to ask you the same question. Has she come here before?"

Marcel shook his head; he didn't move.

"Eh, Marcel! Du pain! Du pain! Toute de suite!"

It was the patron.

"Merde!" hissed Marcel, as he ran to the kitchen in the back.

I can't remember eating the omelet.

Pour out, my lady, and I shall drink all that you offer.

The girl, who now sat opposite me, was Helena's image. I had never thought to see that face in the waking world.

I felt that my wanderings were over.

This was my Isabelle.

It was slowly, at first, that she let me enter her life. She came from Mantes-la-Jolie, a little city just west of Paris on the Grande Ligne. She had just finished studying design at college and was now working for a jewelry company in Paris.

Her words, her laughter, her tenderness were a flood across my barren heart.

That first day, I was her guide through Rouen. I remember she laughed at the gaping, retching, defecating gargoyles on the Church of Saint-Maclou.

"Why do churches have these monsters outside?" Without my realizing it, her arm had slipped through mine.

"Perhaps because holy places are surrounded by the world, which is profane."

"And the world is also beautiful."

She turned up her face towards me, and I saw how dark her eyes were, and how softly her brown hair curled against her cheeks.

It seemed quite natural to kiss her, and when she returned the kiss, and her arms came around me, I felt not so much passion as homecoming — to Ithaca, for which all wanderers yearn.

Those early days with Isabelle were filled only with laughter and with bliss.

In time, she moved to Rouen, and she spurred me to look for better-paying jobs. We were inseparable.

Some nights, we would talk about our plans, about the places we'd see together. She wanted to see America and India. I told her all I could about America, with its expanse of land that is incomprehensible to Europeans, the wide, open roads; the crisp beauty of autumn. About India I had much to say, but no real memories of my own.

I realize now that I was the same dream-spinner I had been as a child, with blue-eyed Cynthia. I would talk about that distant place of my origins, the land by whose rivers the Aryans gave up their nomadic ways and became city-dwellers, though they kept the memory of their wanderings alive in exuberant hymns. The land where Alexander lost his beloved horse Bucephalus, around whose pyre he built a city, the ruins of which can still be seen today. The land where the Buddha himself preached, whose carved images show him dressed like a Greek philosopher. The land ravaged by Tamerlane. The land from where the Mughal hegemony began. The land of Sufis, mystics, saints, warriors. A land where wheat fields undulated like a golden sea beneath the arid, blue sky. A land of blood and honour, where men in chain-mail still rode out on horses with ancient swords strapped to their sides. A hard land where ordinary people could quote reams of poetry. A land so distant from me, yet still so close . . .

And as we talked, Isabelle would curl up close to me on the sofa, and her long hair fell like a darkness upon her shoulders and her back, and the beauty of her face was like an oasis in that house on rue Bouquet, where we now lived, a place already filled with our dreams and our hope.

With her leaning on my shoulder, we would lapse into silence, because words were no longer needed; presence and touch were sufficient.

When we had talked the moon down, Isabelle would go to bed, and I would tell her that I'd follow soon after.

I would get up to draw the curtains. The thoroughfare was busy as ever; a man might be struggling and kicking at the condom-vending machine by the corner where the red light district began, while an impatient hooker stood nearby; a police car might cruise slowly, and a black Maria race off, past the station.

No city of lights this; yet a place I had come to call home. And there was an oasis, too, next door to us. My elderly neighbours, Pierette and Gilles MacDougall, tended a tiny, vibrant garden, alive with bird song, where a little fountain in the shape of a squatting bear sputtered all day long. Gilles hailed from an old line of Scottish emigrants that had accompanied Bonnie Prince Charlie on his sojourn.

I marvelled at their ability to coax such a variety of shrubs, flowers, and ornamental grasses in that little patch of earth. It was an Eden beside Gomorrah.

Pierrette's pride and joy was a potted orange tree. They had visited their son, their only child, in Greece a few years back, and he had taken them to an orange grove. Pierette had never seen anything like it, she said. She'd nearly squealed with delight when her son picked a ripe orange and handed it to her. Right there and then, she peeled back the thick, golden skin, and the first taste of that orange would stay with her all her life. She saved the pips, and brought them home with her. And one of those pips had become the tree she so tenderly cared for.

We lived in that house on rue Bourquet for nearly three years, and we watched that tree become bigger, stronger, and thicker. Pierrette's only regret was that it bore no fruit. Still, she tended it with an almost maternal love, taking it indoors whenever a cold wind blew, singing to it even, or so it seemed to me, when she was out in her garden, always the same song: *"Quand il me prend dans ses bras, Il me parle tout bas . . . "*

One day, as Isabelle and I passed by their door, she excitedly waved an envelope in the air.

"Our son — he's coming to visit! And look over there, just look!"

The orange tree had yielded to her love; it was filled with small, white flowers, pale yellow in the centre.

One night, Isabelle curled up beside me, handed me a glass of calvados, in which she had put a sugar cube, and said:

"Tell me your earliest memory."

"My first memory?" I asked, taking a sip and feeling the liquor make the famous *le trou Normand*, or the "Norman hole" — the true test of good calvados — the clearing of the passage from the mouth all the way down to the gut.

"Your very earliest memories, when you were a child."

I put down my drink, held her close, and told her what I remembered.

I am in my mother's lap; I am a year or so old. I am squirming around a lot. Suddenly I lunge forward and smash my face against a glass. The water turns red. My mother cries with me. I have the scar still below my left eye. Then, I am a little older, and my sister and I are playing on some swings. I am clumsy and fall, cutting myself just above my left eye. My sister, a child herself, doesn't know what to do. She has a little handkerchief that she presses over my cut. That scar is now hidden beneath my eyebrow. When I was born, at home, the midwife didn't tie my umbilical cord tight enough. It was a little while later when my grandmother picked me up that she found me covered in blood. I can recall still a feeling of ebbing away, slowly, towards a darkness that was all my own . . .

Isabelle softly stroked my hair; her hand had a fragrance that I could not name.

"Tell me more."

I picked up the drink; the sugar cube had nearly dissolved.

I remember being hungry. We have no money. But I do not cry. We make no demands, though we have nothing. I cannot even imagine what kind of toys I would want, if I were given the chance to ask. We laugh. My mother gets food on credit . . .

My sister looks after me when I am ill, during the day. At night, I lie beside my mother. It is dark. I am afraid. Softly, I hear her crying, sniffing away the tears. I cling to her; she holds me tight. Her hands seem so much bigger than mine . . .

In the mornings, she carries me to keep me warm. My sister and brother do not go to school; there is no money for the fees. But my brother still gets dressed in his school clothes early in the morning, climbs to the flat rooftop, where we sleep in the summer, and reads. In my bed, I look at comic books that he has borrowed from friends. I cannot read, but I like the pictures; the colours soothe my fever. I look at drawings of cars, picnics, waterfalls, animals dressed like people. My eyes are hot and burning. I put down the comic book and listen to my mother cleaning the house; she sings as she works. Her voice is a cavern of hope . . .

The sugar cube had completely disappeared in the brandy, but I drank no more.

Instead, I put my head in Isabelle's lap, and with her quiet hands, she stroked my hair, my face, my neck.

She let out a little cry — her hands were wet. It was the first time that I wept in a woman's lap.

Later, I went through the house and made sure the lights were off, and the doors locked. I looked through the curtains: the McDougall's house lay dark and quiet, and in Pierrette's little garden, I could see the orange tree, the white flowers catching a streetlight's gleam.

I went up to the bedroom. Isabelle was fast asleep. I softly closed the door.

The shadowy glow of the city poured through the bedroom window and caught her sleeping form. Her hair fell like a veil across her face; her bare shoulder gleamed faintly.

I looked at her, not moving, scarcely thinking.

Despite the gargoyles that mock and mimic the fringes of human lives, the centre is pure, holy. I had found my Penelope at last.

As I got in beside her, she stirred and turned to lie close against me. There again was that fragrance that I could not name.

I closed my eyes. And before I fell asleep, I promised I would show her the two countries she'd wanted to see.

One day, we would watch snow fall quietly among thick forests of pine, and one day, too, we would stand in the mist of the high Himalayas and watch the Ganges descend, whose waters must wash away the sins of so many lives . . .

Journal Entry: Half a Loaf of Bread

When I was a child, my teachers and my family were certain that I would amount to a lot; but nothing grand happened. All I had ever done well was build a cocoon around myself, a cocoon with many layers: distant lands, ancient times, comic-book heroes. With Isabelle, I have learned to live outside my cocoon, where I have the surety of ordinary life. I consciously fill each day so it will not flit away unused.

I still get the urge to move on, sometimes, but Isabelle and I have our dreams to fulfill — I shall not be alone.

I have outgrown the duality of wanderers: they seek permanence of place, yet perpetually move on to avoid it. They walk in silence, exploring the world that lies beneath their feet, while they themselves are lost in the labyrinth of their hearts. And slowly dust settles where they once sat. No one knows they came, stayed a little while, and then moved on.

Alone here, in another rainy city, I feel only half myself. For these four months Isabelle and I, who have scarcely been a day out of each other's company, will only be voices on the telephone: she in Lille, taking the fashion design course, and myself here in London, representing Lauzon Investments. As an Anglophone, I am valuable to them: it was the main reason they gave me the job.

Yes, we are ambitious now, Isabelle and I — we are "knuckling down" as the English say. To make our life together, to follow our dreams of travel and exploration, we must leave the carefree fringes of society for a spell. In short, we must save money!

My rooms are in a little red brick house across from the "tube" station where I travel each day to the City. It is a depressing enough location, yet just fifteen minutes from my flat, up the steep, narrow street, is a large park — some solace to me in my few spare hours. I take a book with me, or sometimes just sit and absorb.

And indeed, London — for all its grime and congestion — has a magic of its own. It was the hub of the world once, and the echoes of that time still linger. I have walked down the street where Rimbaud and Verlaine lost their way; sat in the museum where Marx researched his *Kapital*; passed the law school where Tagore abandoned his studies. It seems to me sometimes that London is overwhelmed by its ghosts. Yet the living have their stories to tell, too.

Half way up the street towards the park stands a house in which the German theologian, Dietrich Bonhoeffer, lived during his stay in London. It was a small brick house, similar to the one in which I had my room.

The first day as I went up the hill, I stopped to read the commemorative plaque by its front door. Bonhoeffer knew that passivity can easily become complicity, and therefore powerless before evil. In 1935, he became the leader of the Confessing Church of Germany, which sought the overthrow of Hitler. He fought evil with his words, but conviction demands sacrifice. He was arrested by the Gestapo in April of 1943. And he underwent his own Passion, torture, temptation, fear, and doubt. But he did not forsake his faith — he, too, would give his head, but not his essence. In Schoenberg Prison, in Flossenburg, on Monday Apirl 9, 1945, he was led from his cell into the courtyard, and stripped naked — it was a raw spring day. It is said that he took off his glasses, mounted the gallows, and was hanged. Just one week later, the Allies entered Flossenberg.

He believed that by overcoming evil in his own life, evil could be overcome in life itself. When he was led away to his execution, he said to a fellow prisoner: "This is the end, but for me the beginning of life."

Walking on up the hill, towards the haven of the park, I recalled the mindless cruelty the Nazis perpetrated in their pursuit of superiority. The very first victims of their methodical destruction of humanity were not Jews, but a group of almost a thousand Gypsy children. No one cared what happened to Gypsies, with their origins in northern India, they were no better than weeds in the eyes of most Europeans, and for the Nazis, this was a practice run that no one would notice — for the horrors to come.

The ashes of these children were collected and made into soap, which was then distributed to their own mothers. The women were happy to receive the soap, thinking they could finally clean themselves. But when they were told how the soap was actually made, they wailed and wept in their uncomprehending sorrow, and then gently kissed those little grey bars, as if they were their children's precious, lost bodies . . .

Who will ever atone for all those sins . . . ?

I passed the houses, which line the park, and chose a bench beneath a beech tree. Lovers had carved their initials on its grey bark: GD + MO FOREVER.

It was a warm day for January, with clouds that the wind hustled around. I opened my book and immersed myself in the world of Empedocles and his pre-Socratic friends.

The wind bared the sky, and the sun showed through like a pale ball of curd draining in gauze.

Empedocles was busy defining the nature of being as the blending and unblending of primordial matter, or what India calls the cycle of birth, death and re-birth. Blending is birth, and when that blending becomes unglued and falls apart that is "sad-ordained death." In their simplicity, men say that existence comes into being from nothing, Empedocles was telling me with a smirk, and men believe that in death existence vanishes into unknown darkness. The truth, he told me, was that matter moved in a great cycle, forming and unforming, assuming countless shapes. Nothing died in reality, but re-appeared, changed, in a different guise, under another name. Existence was fixed upon the wheel of being, from which emerged the world and the universe alike, in endless play, now appearing, now disappearing, like a camera lens moving in and out of focus. If you thought like that, there was no fear in death, for the greatest fear is the annihilation of the self. But if the deathless self took on endless shapes within creation, where was the fear? Death was merely an unblending of light, earth, air, water and fire. Birth and life were reversals of this action. This was eternity's great circle. In my mind, I was making connections between Empedocles and Vedic cosmology.

When I looked up from my woolgathering, I found I had a companion on the bench; an old woman, lightly holding the crook of a pale wooden cane. She was looking across the green expanse of the park, as if searching for something.

I said hello, and she smiled and asked me what I was reading so intently.

"Actually, it's a book on Greek philosophy," I told her rather apologetically. It's embarrassing being caught reading a pretentious book of this sort, in public.

Her face was thin and wan; wisps of fine, white hair were picked up by the wind. With bony, cramped hands, she brushed them back into place. Her eyes were a pale grey, like the sky that day. She laid her cane in her lap and nodded with a smile.

"Ah yes, philosophy," she said, "an intriguing subject for the mind, I must say."

"It keeps me occupied," I replied.

"I studied philosophy when I was young. At Oxford, you know. There were very few women in university in those days. Most got married, had children, and settled into their lives." She let out a light laugh, picked up the cane, and jabbed at the soil beside her foot.

"But that was not for me. I caused my poor father no end of concern. I do believe I was a tomboy of sorts when I was a young girl. I could be found forever swinging from trees, scrambling amongst the branches. How many times I came home with cuts and bruises, but happy. And my mother would scold me gently, saying that proper young girls did not do these kinds of things. But I told her that it was jolly good fun to climb to the top of a tree and look all around."

She slowly straightened out her legs and fixed her hair again.

"My father was a stern man, but with a very gentle heart. I never remember him scolding me at all. Whenever I walked into the room, he smiled; indeed he could barely conceal that smile, even when it needed concealing — when I had been especially riotous and come home with a muddied dress, or my boots all scuffed. Certainly, it was my mother who was the disciplinarian in the family. But I knew how to get around her."

She laughed and shook her head, then looked towards the houses beyond.

"I live with my son, you know, and his wife; she doesn't like me very much, I am sorry to say. She will soon be free of me, however." She laughed again, but softly, sadly, and didn't meet my eyes.

"Now where was I? Oh yes. My first year at Oxford, I took logic; and the first problem given to us stated: logic can prove that half a loaf of bread is better than heaven. Let's look after the here-and-now, and leave the hereafter to worry about itself." Her voice trailed off and she looked up at a nearby tree, where a thrush sat warbling, its throat swollen with the repeated notes of its song.

There was a rich tenor to her voice, which few listened to, I guessed. There was a naïve sincerity to her words, and she spoke as if I were no stranger.

"Isn't logic a wonderful thing?" she asked, then continued, without waiting for a reply.

"You know, I have one great regret in my life. I was never able to instill a belief in heaven in my only son. He tells me that he doubts God exists, something which I find rather prevalent nowadays, without reason really; simply because it's fashionable, I suppose. Most people don't think about things like religion. My son saddens me, you know, especially now that I am an old woman and confronting my own mortality, as it were. I wish I could have given my son a faith in the hereafter." She was poking at the earth again with her cane, a perplexed expression on her face.

Her shoulders stooped as she leaned back on the bench. Her face still bore traces of beauty from her youth. She closed her eyes when she smiled, I noticed. A habit from her childhood?

After a little pause, she asked me the time.

"A little before noon," I told her.

"Time for lunch, then, it is. My daughter-in-law does not like me to be late for lunch or dinner, or breakfast for that matter."

She shuffled her feet slightly; then straightened her back.

"She always tells me, 'What's the point of preparing something hot when you're just going to let it go cold.' Good logic that, wouldn't you say? But I must go."

Her eyes closed and she gave me that little smile.

She gripped the pommel of her cane with both hands and got herself up with a laboured push. I, too, got on my feet to give her a hand.

A group of children ran around our bench, laughing and screeching before rushing off to the green, chasing nothing in particular but themselves.

"Be careful, children," she called after them and laughed feebly. Was she seeing herself on that greensward, the tomboy, heedless of her mother's scolding?

"Well, I wish you the best, young man," she said, "I have lunch to go to. We can't have it go cold now, can we?"

I wished her a good afternoon and watched her walk slowly away, leaning on her cane.

It took her a while to reach the other side of the green, following the direction of the running children earlier . . .

I do not know if half a loaf of bread is better than heaven. The cloud of unknowing is the end of logic.

Journal Entry: Eugenia

The wind lashed rain like a myriad whips outside. In these storms, roofs were blown away, people knocked down, trains cancelled because of flooded tracks, and roads made impassable.

From my window, I followed the patterns the wind etched on puddles and just as quickly snatched away as it moved on. My windowpane was a flimsy shield against the chaos outside.

How different the rain was here in London from that which fell on Rouen. And I missed that rain. There, it was an overflowing of clouds; here, it was a wild torrent, a howling gush.

When I told this to Isabelle on the phone, she laughed at me, demanding how could I become sentimental over rain, of all things — and what about her? But when I told her that English bread was all crumb and no crust, she told me, in feigned indignation, to come home right away. However, I did not have to stay long, just a few days more, and then back to Rouen.

We talked for a long time; I clung to her voice. An emptiness overtook me as we said goodbye and I hung up the telephone.

There was a knock on the door.

It was Eugenia standing there, arms folded demurely.

"Have you made your daily phone call?"

I told her I had.

"Do you feel any better?"

I told her either to come in or to leave. She laughed and stepped into the room.

Eugenia was from Gijón and had come to London, like many others, to learn English. To support herself, she worked in the café at the British Museum. And since the trains were cancelled that day, she had stayed home.

"It is just as well. I have to finish some manuscripts."

She was also a reader for a small literary agency that specialized in trashy novels; this too she did to improve her English.

The museum's café where she worked was just down the hall from the gallery for Greek pottery. And if I happened to be in the vicinity, I would drop in and have a coffee, and then sit amid the ruins and fragments of forgotten lives.

Homer and the Greeks were my first love; that is what I told Isabelle, and she invariably responded with a Greek-shepherd-and-his-sheep joke. But she well knew my fascination with that dry land of the Hellenes, which gave rise to ideas that created the world we live in, even today. And beyond these patterns was a deeper structure, hidden but not forgotten — ideas, mythic patterns, even specific words that Greece and India shared, and this affinity stretched out to include the Germanic, Celtic, Slavic, Baltic, and Italic cultures. It is said that a person who knows Sanskrit can easily understand Lithuanian, so close is the similarity. And further back, there was the connection with the Hittites, whose word for "water" is exactly the same as the English. Close neighbours of the Hittites were the Mitannians, the first recorded group of Indo-Aryans, whose chiefs bore names that would later define the culture of India — Varuna, Mitra, Indra. But these tribes would not wander east towards the Punjab for another five hundred years. The most famous Mitannian is Nefertiti, the wife of Akhenaten, and mother of Tutankhamun.

Sitting in that gallery, I would imagine what the ancient Greeks would make of my life. A taut harmony? Two opposites pulling away from each other, creating a space in between, like a bowstring — middle-air — that balanced ether and earth, the world of the gods and the world of men. How mute are images when those that love them are gone.

One day, Isabelle gave me a poem she had written, after the style of Sappho; I set it to memory, and know it even today:

Sweet Hesperos, distant, most beautiful,
you gather what the hurrying sun
flung far and near.
A round dance in stone:
I have neither the honey nor the bee,
and no sacred groves, smoking with incense,
await the arrival of a deep-clouded god —
only the hurrying plow,
and the new blown hyacinth,
cut purple upon the furrow . . .

There are so many roads that one can follow. If we take just one, we end up inside ourselves and find that our souls are wisps of silence and emptiness shaped by the skin of mystery, which some call breath, others the oscillation of the heavenly spheres.

I, too, had many roads to follow.

The one I took has led me to Isabelle; and now I can sit at the crossroads and watch others walk on, for I have found my destination. And the days may come and go like clouds in the deep blue sky that sends down rain, snow, thunder, and light in their season.

Last summer was a busy one for Isabelle and me. We drove from one end of France to the other, following the Atlantic coastline, taking an impromptu tour of the vineyards of Bordeaux, stopping at some small winery, buying a few bottles and then moving on. We promised ourselves that, in time, we would move about the world more, breathing the air of different lands, basking under distant suns. That summer we ended up on some dusty back road that sooner or later led to a small village, where shepherds made their own cheese and dry-sausage, where the bread was big and round, with a hard crust that you first dipped in water before eating, and where the wine they offered us was thick and heady, some even made from wild grapes.

We were headed for the Pyrenees. With every kilometer, we scanned the horizon, waiting for the mountains to loom suddenly.

It was early morning when we reached Bayonne. The sun was just beginning to break. We got out of the car and gazed up at the mountains — smooth and jagged, thrusting high — that changed with the light and the clouds, minute by minute. Just across them was Spain. Behind us, all of France. I put my arms around Isabelle and said nothing. Words were useless.

She whispered that she would never leave me . . .

The rainstorms continued, and the trains were perpetually cancelled. I did most of my work over the telephone, writing out my reports, and sending them to Paris by courier.

Since Eugenia was also mostly at home, she brought her work over to my room. We both needed companionship, being ex-patriots of sorts. While we had coffee, she would read her lurid manuscript of the week, while I plotted bond ratings, gains and losses.

On this last night she'd brought a typescript that was carefully bound in cardboard from a Corn Flakes cereal box; it was entitled "Harem Fantasy." She made me read it; and when I had finished (it took about an hour), she asked me what I thought. I told her the sex was English, but the prose wasn't. This delighted her to no end, and she wrote that comment in her reader's report. I told her to be kind; it was probably some person's dream she was smashing. But that only made her more determined to write a carefully worded, devastating review of the manuscript. I sincerely felt sorry for the would-be author. Then she went back to her place to type up what she had written.

She asked me to come to dinner. I went out, bought a bottle of wine, and showed up. As we ate and drank, she told me about the Asturias, of her city, of her family, of the heat of summer. She gestured strongly with her hands, and bobbed her head rapidly, if she wanted you to agree with what she said.

"Do you know, every summer, my mother dries hundreds of tomatoes in the sun, and strings garlic to make lumpy garlands."

And later, "My father teaches physics, but my mother taught me many songs. Do you want me to sing you one?"

I said that it would be a rare pleasure.

When she sang her voice was clear, unwavering; her hands waved with each phrase; she had lifted up her face and closed her eyes, and as she sang, her throat slightly trembled. She sang a song she'd learned as a child from a group of Gypsies:

For the love of horses, my love,
you strove across this strong black earth.
For the love of wealth, my love,
you sailed across the deepest seas.
For the love of kingdoms, my love,
you learned to sit upon flashing thrones.
For the love of heaven, my love,
you gave bright gold in charity.
But when I came to you, my love,
you had nothing left to give.
From my heart you drank red wine, my love,
and emptied, you sent me far away.

She told me how these Gypsies danced beneath sun-washed porticoes: the flash of blue, green, crimson, orange; the fragrance of saffron slowly releasing its colour in milk; the wildness of laments; and the sudden clap of hands as the dancer, caught in a burst of colour and sound, stopped, her eyes closed, hands held high, filled with beauty; the world is before her, destroyed; her dancing will again bring it shape, return it, transformed, enlivened to the audience; the tight strum of the guitar; her hands undulate; and all is as it should be. Movement and not stillness; joyous shouting and not silence.

The next day, Eugenia phoned me early. The rains had subsided and I was planning to go into central London. Her voice was dry and her words hesitant.

"My mother. Something has happened." she blurted out. "I must go back to Gijón. I must."

I went over to her room, and she opened the door before I could knock. There were hurriedly dried tears on her face. I embraced her.

Holding me tight, she said, "My father says she is dying. I must hurry."

And with great, heaving sobs she wept against me, her tears warm upon me.

We stood there for a very long time.

That day, I helped her pack.

While she was fastening a buckle on her suitcase, she looked up at me suddenly and said:

"I don't even know English very well."

Eugenia left that night. I got a taxi and went with her to the airport. It was about an hour's drive, and we travelled in silence. Looking out the window, she wiped frequent tears. She was twenty years old.

I took the tube home, and phoned Isabelle. It was a long call. I couldn't wait to get out of England. I had only two more days left.

And then my work was finished, and I stood in Victoria Station waiting to board the train for Newhaven, and back to France.

By mid-afternoon I was in Paris. I could again relish the bread, the food, and there was Isabelle to come home to!

That very day I was in my room on rue Puits. Cheerfully, I walked again the streets of Rouen, and inhaled deeply — the air was not bitter from exhaust fumes as in London.

The next day, I drove out to Lille.

And there I found the embrace for which I had yearned all those days, the laughter, the smile, the fragrance of skin, the light of the sun on hair, the alluring walk, the neatly painted toenails, the happy eyes, the clear forehead — Isabelle's love. And I lost myself completely in her for the next week.

From Lille, I did send a note of sympathy to Eugenia, asking her to let me know how things were, and how she was faring. Was she looking after herself? Was she coping well with everything? And that she was welcome to come and stay with us in Rouen if she needed to.

I gave her our Rouen address and telephone, Isabelle's address and telephone in Lille, and even my office address and telephone at Lauzon's. Weeks passed, and then months. I heard nothing from her. I wrote again. Nothing. Then I telephoned and asked about her in my broken Spanish. The person who answered did not identify himself; I let Isabelle talk because her Spanish was more fluent than mine, and because she was a woman. The man on the other end was Eugenia's brother. And yes, their mother died two months ago. Eugenia was living with some cousins in the countryside. Yes, they had received my letter, for which they thanked me, and they would tell Eugenia that I telephoned. I never heard from Eugenia again.

Sometimes, like today, when I remember her voice, I think of writing or telephoning her, but never do in the end nor, I suppose, ever will. How do you enter a life once you've left it?

CHAPTER 11

IT WAS NEARLY THE END OF OCTOBER; the wind from the Himalayas carried with it the chill of distant snows. People walked about huddled under thick woolen shawls bearing patterns particular to their region: crisscrossing diamond shapes and intersecting squares, coloured a deep burgundy, mauve, and green.

Like all other houses in the village, we had a large brazier in the middle of our rooms, where we fired coals to warm the air inside; there was no fear of carbon monoxide because of the large vents that slit the walls three feet down from the roof: there was always a draft, and the warmth of course quickly escaped. But we kept comfortable.

Punjab is a land of extremes. In the summer the temperature soars up to 50°C and then the earth is arid and parched, and the air filled with fine, dry, searing dust that whips the face with each gust of wind; it is a Mediterranean dryness found nowhere else in India. But in the winter the temperature dips to below freezing, where a sudden downpour of rain can leave you covered in a fine film of ice.

The Lohri festival was not far off, now, when bonfires are lit, and children go from house to house asking for treats. Legend has it that the eighteenth-century robber baron, Dulla Bhatti, began this celebration when he secretly married a Muslim man and a Hindu girl in his forest hideout. The families of the couple opposed the marriage, so the lovers sought out Dulla's help. He had no qualms about religion and said love must transcend difference — if only modern India had been ruled by such men.

It was at this time that Bawa-ji chose to be on his way. He had stayed almost as long in Dhanoa as I had; now he made preparations for his winter sojourn. He would wend his way to Jwalamukhi, where flames from deep magma shoot up through crevices and are worshipped as manifestations of the Great Goddess. Then he would travel further up to the mountains towards Hrishikesh, the glacier sacred to Shiva, and the birthplace of the river Ganges, which is said to flow from the god's long hair.

"Why go to the mountains in winter?" I asked him. People usually took to the hills during summer for some cooler weather; the Himalayas were treacherous during winter.

"My friend, I always go to the mountains in the winter because the snow reminds me so much of Kabul. One day, I shall keep walking — never mind the borders — and I shall end up in that city of my childhood. I still have some family there, but it's been so long since I have seen them." He smiled, as he slowly began to roll his fawn-skin mat.

"There is a temple in Kabul dedicated to Sri Chand, the founder of our sect. Despite all the wars and bombs in Afghanistan, it still stands. Yes, one day I shall see Kabul again. Our house was near Shor Bazaar."

The skin on his neck was loose and deeply wrinkled, and I noticed, as if for the first time, how gaunt his hands were, and how frail.

"I am the last one left who can still remember our days in Kabul," Bawa-ji said.

"After I became a *saadh*, my younger brother educated himself in India and became a doctor. Then he left for America; he is doing very well in New York. But he never came back. India was not his home; just as it is not mine. Our true homeland we cannot go back to. What is there left to do but wander?"

Bawa-ji's voice seemed weary. The twinkle had gone from his eyes.

He picked up his staff and leaned on it heavily. "Eventually, my parents, too, went to America, along with my sister and two other brothers. My brothers and sister married Americans and are now full natives of that land. My father died five years ago; my mother is still alive. I write to her regularly, even though she cannot reply since I have no fixed address. I know my father wanted to see Kabul again. How he loved springtime there — with the blossoming cherry trees, the wild lilacs, and the jasmine. Despite all the horror and the bloodshed in Afghanistan now, I know every spring the flowers return with their fragrance. They bring the memory of a gentler era when we were children, and it was time to put on new clothes for the first day of school . . . "

His voice trailed off, as he tied up his sack of belongings, and slung it over his back. The cooing of pigeons floated above us.

I went inside to tell Raj that Bawa-ji was leaving us.

Raj was still in bed. It was well past ten in the morning. He was the early riser, and I forever late out of bed.

I went into his room with a jest on my lips.

When I touched his shoulder, he did not stir.

I shook him a little harder and he rolled over onto his back. His half-closed eyes were a dark red; thin trickles of blood oozed from his nostrils and mouth. He did not respond to my calls or shakings.

I rushed outside; told Bawa-ji what I saw; he dropped everything and hurried into the house.

"Get the doctor from Manali!" His voice was commanding now, strong. "Go! Amarnath will take you. He's still at home." Bawa-ji disappeared into the room.

I ran to the village to fetch Amarnath; I could see his grain truck by the general store. He usually left around eleven o'clock.

I saw Amarnath carry out a sack of grain.

"Raj is very sick. I need to get Dr. Hari Lall!" I shouted as I ran towards him.

"Get in then and let's be on our way!" Amarnath dropped the sack and hopped into the truck, and revved the engine hard.

We roared off in a cloud of dust and barking dogs.

We didn't talk much on the way; no doubt Amarnath was used to long, silent rides in his truck. Cows and buffaloes stood in fields around high-heaped byres, contentedly chewing their cuds. Their placidity contrasted with our wild rush.

Amarnath was a good driver; he careened expertly along narrow roads that were no more than country lanes.

Manali sat perched among the mountains like a mishmash of mud-coloured squares, domes and precarious towers; it was a wonder-filled example of eastern confusion that nevertheless manages to plod along and function rather smoothly, despite the ubiquitous disorder.

We had to go into the centre of the city, to the street of the booksellers, where Dr. Lall had his office.

Amarnath parked his truck beside a little eatery. "We can go quicker by foot."

He jumped down from the cab.

We hurried through a warren of small, narrow alcoves where merchants sold everything from coloured glass bangles, roasted pine nuts, variegated stacks of cloth, sweetly smoking incense, to spears, bright-bladed swords, and gods.

We passed from one narrow alleyway to the next, each darker than the last, where the sun seldom reached because of the overhang of ancient houses, with their intricately carved wooden doors and lintels. The smell of scalding milk and roasting anise was heavy around us, and as we moved deeper into the city the aroma of onions and garlic frying in butter mingled with the sharp odour of stale urine.

The narrow alleys widened, and Amarnath's large hand pulled me towards a wooden door that bore a brass plaque: Dr. Hari Lall, B.Sc. (Hons.), MD, and in curlicue brackets, the phrase, {London Returned}, meaning that our good doctor had been to London and back. In the early years of the last century this phrase was an impressive qualification in the Punjab; presumably it still held good.

We burst through the door.

The waiting room was large and airy, with long, worn-out benches that looked like Church pews, on which about a dozen patients sat, with a look that only the sick carry: one of extreme fatigue, impatience, and hope.

The nurse, a heavy-set woman in a white and pale blue *shulwaar-kameez*, asked us to wait for the doctor.

"But nurse," I said, "there's an emergency in our village!"

"Can we speak with the doctor?" Amarnath planted his great hands on her desk.

She did not seem impressed.

"I doubt the doctor-sahib will go with you on such a short notice," she informed us in a bored voice; no doubt she'd heard these demands frequently.

"Why didn't you bring the patient with you?" she added with a sarcastic smile.

"The patient can't be moved! Just let me speak to the doctor!" I was nearly shouting.

The dozen or so patients in the waiting room gave us hostile stares, marking us as impertinent queue-jumpers.

But my words only hardened the nurse's resolve to follow procedure, right down to the letter — something hardly ever done in India.

"The doctor is busy. You'll just have to wait." She flung these words over her shoulder, as she disappeared into another room.

Anxiously, we went and sat down among the patients, who frowned at us; some smiled with satisfaction.

The bench on which I sat bore a little silver plaque on its armrest, which read: "7th Punjab Rifles. Mess." This was the regiment that had fought heroically against the Japanese in Burma. How the mighty have fallen . . .

It took a very long time, in fact, for the doctor's door to open. And when it did, we both shot up.

But someone else came out. A young man in his twenties. Dr. Mehta. He was an intern with Dr. Lall, who had gone off to New Delhi to some conference and would not be back for another four days.

Quickly, we explained our situation. Could he possibly come up to Dhanoa? He was really busy, he said, as we could see, but he would speed things up as best he could, and then come with us.

We waited another two hours before he came out again, following the last patient. We hurried him along,

189

helping him with his jacket, and Amarnath took up his bag.

We made our way back to the truck. It was now 2:30 in the afternoon — almost five hours since we left Dhanoa.

Amarnath drove right up to Raj's house.

We found Bawa-ji in the courtyard, sitting on the cot beneath the mulberry tree, telling his beads methodically. All around him stood the men of the village, as well as some children, whom I recognized as Raj's students.

Bawa-ji got up when he saw us, and walked over.

"Raj Kumar has ascended." His voice was barely a whisper.

The doctor, Amarnath, and I went inside the room.

Raj lay on the dirt floor near the door. He was already wound in a clean white sheet. A clay lamp burned slowly near his head; an overpowering perfume of ambergris incense hung in the room.

When the last minutes approached, Bawa-ji had lifted Raj from his bed and laid him on the stamped dirt floor — in accordance with Hindu and Sikh tradition — so he could die in the lap of mother earth.

Raj looked so frail, like a child that has lost something and doesn't know where to start looking. A thin strip of cloth passed under his chin and was tied over his head.

"Who was he?" Dr. Mehta asked me.

"Raj Kumar — my friend," I tried to keep my voice from cracking.

"Would you like me to determine the cause of death?" asked the young doctor.

I could only nod.

Then, I went outside and sat down beside Bawa-ji.

Amarnath came and sat beside me, his great shoulders slumped forward.

"So, you will leave today for Jwalamukhi, Bawa-ji," I asked him.

"Yes . . . " he answered.

After a long silence, Bawa-ji pointed to the horizon.

"Look," he said.

A long, white line of cranes was flying South, returning to warmer feeding grounds for the winter. They were flying down from Russia, having passed over Kabul.

As we watched, two more cranes flew up from the apricot grove, their haunting, long cries hovering in the still air. They glided off, elegantly plying the air. We watched them float effortlessly away, their lissome wings swaying, dark and soft grey.

They, too, were leaving Dhanoa; they would never again hear the children repeating their lessons, or singing those French songs.

Deva Singh and Raj's music pupils entered the courtyard and, without speaking, laid down a rug, took out their instruments, tuned them, and began to play. They sang the words of Kabir, India's greatest mystic.

Tears welled in my eyes at the plaintive words and the supple melody, and I wept for my friend who left without saying farewell . . .

Seeing the gardener,
the buds cried out:
'He has picked all the flowers;
now he comes for us.'

Journal Entry: Maya

And the time came that Isabelle and I bought our house, a place that would carry our signature, our stamp for all the world to see.

Isabelle had established herself with creative designs, not just in jewelry but also pottery, for Rouen is the home of the best faience; its reputation goes back to the Middle Ages. My own work had led me to bigger firms, who actually followed my opinions and advice about things financial.

When we moved into our house, spring was just beginning, and the rain had stopped long enough to facilitate our move. Isabelle was meticulous in arranging: the sofa, the lounge chairs, the shelves, the kitchen table, the bed, even the clothes in the closet. Her sense of order greatly impressed me that day. I kept myself out of the way by sticking to what I knew best — lugging.

By the time everything was laid out as she wanted, it was well past midnight, and we hadn't eaten all day. We had some bread and cheese and a glass of wine, and then off to bed.

But in the end, everything is illusion. We are all in the grip of Maya, whose strength even the gods cannot thwart. Speak stones, palaces, streets. Loosen, words, O cities eternal, for all is now quiet with me. Cry out, trees, roadways, churches, mansions, ruins. I have grown tired of words.

In our new house, Isabelle rose early; she had much to do. Swirls of patterns seemed to lie in her hands like fingerprints, which she evoked and translated into beautiful things that people could cherish and pass on to others.

She would sit with me in a meadow and say: "A poppy never blinks." And she would take paper and fill it with images.

But that day, she hurried to get dressed; she didn't have to. She was going to drive to Paris and be back by evening.

Was her mind caught by some Celtic swirl that neither begins nor ends but winds on in symmetry?

Her eyes were clear and dark; her hair was heavy with curls, chestnut brown. The early morning filled with her laughter and her voice warmed the room.

In the years I knew her, I never grew tired of looking at her sleeping form; her breathing reminded me of her patterns which fell back on themselves in order to unfold.

She once said that she dreamt our children would be like us; and I held her close and felt a comfort that I never knew before, nor have known since. Hers was a softness that beckoned me to lay down my loads and forget myself in her arms, slowly taking in her presence like the roots of a tree soaking up water. She called me her Bohemian, softly speaking the words to me: *"Je m'en allais, les poings dans mes poches crevées . . . que d'amours splendides j'ai rêvées . . . "*

Yes, that day, for some reason she rushed to get in the car and drive off to Paris. She would be back by evening, she said, and I was to have dinner ready.

I watched our green car drive off in the early sunlight. Good thing it wasn't raining, I thought. I didn't like her to drive long distances in the rain.

She drove until she reached Mantes-la-Jolie, her hometown; she wanted to have a quick visit with her mother. Her father would probably be at work.

She couldn't find a place to park, so she pulled to the curb, in the French style, right by the house. She wasn't staying too long.

After a quick cup of coffee, she was out the door. She gave her mother a hug, and said that they would meet soon.

As her mother closed the door — a hard screech of wheels, a dull thud of metal against something, a brief scream.

And you, you . . . No! Not yet! Anyone, but you! Our dreams! Why should a mouse have life and you not draw breath . . .

I am back in Rouen, slowly preparing for my day. The phone rings. It is Isabelle's mother; unable to speak.

"Isabelle, Isabelle . . . In the hospital. The doctor. Please, please come quick."

Marcel drives me, as fast as he can, to Mantes-la-Jolie. It takes so long. More than two hours. All these cars. I want to get out and run.

I go to the house first. No one there. A note on the door for me. The location of the hospital. Marcel takes me there.

Everyone is in the waiting room. Her mother, father, and her young brother. All of them with glazed eyes, unbelieving.

The doctor has just left them with the news.

Only her father is able to speak.

"Isabelle. She's gone . . . "

I don't know what to do. I am blind. I would give half my breaths, all my breaths to make her live again. But no one asks me to give.

Holding each other, we go back home.

I am alone in the backyard.

I go to the kitchen, and fill a large glass bowl with water.

And in the empty backyard, I slowly pour out the water on the earth for her thirsty soul.

The salt of my tears is in my mouth. I am like a child to whom much was promised, but nothing given, and that which he had was also taken away.

Where have you vanished so quickly, my love?

I weep the entire day and far into the night.

I don't know when I fall asleep, but when I do, I dream of Isabelle — that she comes to me, standing by my bed. She does not smile, her hair is tied back, and her clothes are all white.

When I try to rise to embrace her, she motions to me to lie still. I can watch only.

With her cold, cold hand, she places on my palm a drop of water.

In my eagerness at seeing her, I cannot hold myself back, and I awake.

My eyes have betrayed me.

I am alone.

Her face living only in my mind. Her voice now lost, unseen, forever . . .

Journal Entry: The Wanderer

I have sold the house in Mont-Sainte-Aignan; the things we carefully gathered I have sold as well. Only some I have kept. Isabelle's things. The ones she cherished most. How cold things are by themselves.

Tomorrow, I shall be leaving this house. A nice, young English couple has bought it. They can't believe how lucky they are to find such a place; and overlooking the Seine valley too. It's perfect for them.

I have packed everything I need. Some clothes, shoes, possessions. I never thought I would leave like this. I am again a wanderer. On whose lap will I rest my head? Where again will I find a piece of earth that I can call my own? Was my Ithaca a dream?

Tonight is my last night here. And also in this city of rains, where so many years of my life have vanished, eaten up by its streets. And aptly enough, today it is gently raining.

The house looks so much bigger now that it's empty. If I cough or clear my throat, the noise echoes.

Marcel will pick me up tomorrow and take me to Mantes-la-Jolie. I have given him our car to keep; a token of our friendship that goes back a long way, back to the time when I first came to Rouen. I will stay with Isabelle's parents for a few days, spend some time, and then move on; I don't know where. Perhaps back to London. Perhaps not. I don't know. I have no more plans. I really do not know what to do any more.

The few books I have are the last things I put in my suitcase. It's strange, after all these years, I am walking

196

away with only two suitcases — just one more than what
I first came with, those long years ago.

Just a few books more. They are wanderers like me;
they come and teach — and then are left behind.

The last one on the shelf is a register, with a black
cover. Isabelle used to write in it. Since there are no chairs
any more, I sit on the floor, and lean against the wall. It
is late. I don't know what time. Night.

I want to write her words out, to draw her to me again.
I dig up a blank pad of paper, get a pen and begin. Her
words again bring me her laughter, which once
brightened these walls like daylight; they bear to me her
body, which once brightened my bed.

On the first page I read, "*Fragments*"; and carefully I
write "*Fragments*" on my pad. My pen begins to follow the
words once traced by her long-fingered hand; yet my
hand is not hers, for hers is now all memory, and mine
living still. And I write out the words slowly, savouring
them, as I once savoured her body:

~~~

And tears were turned to stone, so they would not flow.

~~~

Cold wind, cold wind fly; hours and stars blow by.

~~~

You are no wanderer who,
by stepping inside,
will store up the depths of
dreams and float toward broken trees.

~~~

Bring your words into silence: in throat of earth am I.

~~~

And silence, too, enfolds time, enfolds measure.

~~~

Wind waters eyes

197

> *for all those forever forgotten,*
> *washed of earth*
> *and the sky's deep stain.*

~~~

> *The flower speaks in the seed the riddles of the moon.*

~~~

> *So much singing in emptiness.*

~~~

> *Far away is the first cold gleam of day*
> *when the waters breathe their spray, hearth-heart.*

I can write no more.

Where can I go to lessen my sorrow of you? Tears are not enough.

Long ago, by the grace of your sun, I yielded my own fragments to you, and asked you in unsure words to gather me into your being. Let me again kiss your holy Jordan land; let me comb your hair with the peace of the moon. Bring me your lit candle, radiant, blue as steady stars, which holds your fingers in deathless dance. Look, my words are hollow without you: Come, come again beside me, bring me fire and water. Come, come hold me in your hands, set me alight, and speak of tomorrow's joy.

When I raise my head again, it is dawn, and the empty house around me is now no longer my own.

I wash my face, but my eyes are still red.

Everything is ready. With a numbed heart I wait for Marcel to come and take me away.

By 7:30 he arrives. We greet each other quietly. I leave the house for the last time. I do not look back. I lock the door, put my two suitcases in the trunk and get into the car. The keys to the house I will leave with Marcel; he will give them to the new couple. The sale was private. No agents.

Marcel has the car radio on. I am grateful for the distraction. A voice sings: *Mes yeux dans ton regard* . . .

We are already going down the mountain.

In the somber morning light we leave Rouen behind us.

I turn around for one last look. Familiar Rouen, how many have you known like me? Countless many, yes?

We pick up speed on the highway; only the Seine now running beside us, sparkling golden. My eyes are tired.

How can I say where memory leads? There is only the sudden grasp of recognition. I am leaving this city of rains again, knowing full well that the pattern of return is far, unreadable, perhaps never. And yet surrounding me is you, love, now unsure, unnamed, lost . . .

How can I say where memory leads . . .

Journal Entry: Fragments

So many faces, names, moments vanished behind the veil. Whose eyes have become the perfume of the Lily of the Valley? How many lovers' beauty has the earth's strength broken into dust?

At times I feel the presence of Rouen; I cannot say its pull.

The other day I found again a bishop's seal that I purchased just behind the Church of Saint-Maclou. I had misplaced it; and then suddenly, unexpectedly I found it again. It's a beautiful little gem: no more than two centimeters in diameter, with a one centimeter engraving, in silver, of Mary as the Queen of Heaven, with angels enfolding her in their wings; it is from the seventeenth century. When I found it, I thought again of the day I bought it for a hundred francs; it was late April, just before Isabelle left Rouen forever . . .

If I am in a bookstore, I'll start looking for a book on Normandy; and on the rare occasions that I find one, I look for scenes that I can recognize. An old map of Rouen I have lost, which I regret very much for it was the last thing I had of Isabelle's — perhaps she is that rose that faithfully blooms bright red just by the edge of the apricot grove, drinking the waters of the Piplan Nadi.

Most curious of all, in an antique shop, in New Delhi, I once bought an old French-English dictionary, a constant companion of someone who had lived in France in 1932. It is filled with little notes everywhere.

There is a list of foods that can be cheaply purchased; a list of restaurants with reasonably priced menus; and French terms for common dishes. I imagine this person to be another wanderer, who was in France following in the footsteps of many before him.

At the very back of this dictionary, there is a train schedule for the Grande Ligne, from St. Lazare to Mantes-la-Jolie, to Rouen. How well I knew this very route so many years later.

On the four blank pages at the back, are the words: "The heart is sorrow's eternal nest." And on the inside back cover is inscribed the phrase: "Remembrance is the piety of love."

In the end, even names are no more than words, when the persons who possessed them are gone. But the presence of Rouen, the city of my past labour and love, is perpetual in my life; its mark is stamped upon me. And yet my heart no longer yearns for those things; in the end, I, too, have become another — the past is an abode for memory, wherein none may dwell forever.

My last evocation of Rouen came in the mail: a packet from Marcel, who has not written to me in years.

Long ago, I had written him that I was in Dhanoa.

A flood of words, and even photographs, of himself, of his wife Sandrine, and little daughter, with hair as red as her mother's. He tells me many things: newer buildings all over; some parts I would not even recognize — and that there is a generation growing up in Rouen that could not imagine the city without its Metro. Then he tells me that the house I used to live in burned down last year; the lot is still vacant. I look again at the photographs; smiles and much happiness. I, too, smile.

The letter ends with a warm invitation for me to return to Rouen and visit old friends; there is much to talk about, many years to catch up with, over a slow bottle of wine.

Perhaps today I shall reply to Marcel, and tell him about my new life; even send him some photographs of Dhanoa, the walnut tree, the apricot grove and, if I can, the long lines of cranes flying South.

And perhaps, one day, I shall return to Rouen and feel again its rain and its mist, and hear again my footsteps on its cobbled streets.

How large a circle it is that one must complete in a lifetime, before emerging at the beginning of all things, changed, and yet the same.

And by the waters of the deep-flowing Seine, I shall sit down and throw an offering of golden flowers for the soul of my long-departed love . . .

CHAPTER 12

"WON'T YOU STAY FOR THE FUNERAL?" I asked Bawa-ji.

We sat outside on the cot, where Raj was often found on an evening, and where he spoke of many things: the love poetry of Archilochous, the battles of Cuchulain, supernovas, 1066 and luckless King Harold, the songs of Baba Bulleh Shah. So many things. And now only silence.

Bawa-ji put his hand on my shoulder and spoke reassuringly: "Of course, my friend, of course. Life has no meaning without death. Did you not see the two doves sitting on the roof of the house this morning, cooing ceaselessly. Yamraj, the god of death, had sent his messengers to guide the soul of our friend Raj Kumar to his court. Did you not see them?"

I said I had not, but I had heard them. Doves and pigeons are ill-omened in the Punjab; they are always shooed away.

"I don't know how to read the signs of birds," I answered truthfully.

Bawa-ji continued slowly telling his beads.

By the time Dr. Mehta emerged, the crowd of villagers had grown larger. The men hung their heads in grief; some of the women wept; children looked at their elders in bewilderment.

Someone whispered loudly: "It's a new doctor!"

Hands pressed on his shoulder, faces were poked forward, mouths chattered.

"Doctor-sahib, I've had this lump on my head for two weeks."

"Can you do something with this foot of mine?"

"I think my mare is foaling. Can you spare a minute and look her over?"

Dr. Mehta smiled politely at the press of instant patients, grabbed my elbow, and took me aside.

He had quick inquisitive eyes, and bushy eyebrows that met just above the ridge of his nose.

Hands continued to tug at his shoulders, but he ignored them.

"The cause of death was likely an aneurysm of the brain." He spoke rapidly, his grip on my elbow getting tighter.

"I shall write out the death certificate tomorrow; you can pick it up anytime at the clinic." He shot a glance at the villagers, who stood clamoring for his attention.

"Do you know if he had any family?" Dr. Mehta asked me.

"I don't know. I don't think so. He never mentioned anyone here. Perhaps Bawa-ji knows, or the villagers," I said.

We went over to Bawa-ji, who was deep in conversation with Pundit Prem, the Sikh priest.

The *saadh* shook his head slowly.

"No, Raj Kumar does not have relatives here. His family died in *Vilayat*. He was alone here. He had no one. But we are his family now." He spoke softly. Pundit Prem beside him nodded.

"Well, I'd better get back. Now, where is that fellow that brought us here?"

His single eyebrow shot up, and his eyes searched the crowd for Amarnath.

Then, he quickly turned to me.

"Well, we had better settle the bill. Perhaps you forgot."

I let the insinuation pass, dug into my pocket, and counted off the bills.

He took the money, and without saying anything further, walked out the door.

Several of the villagers ran after him.

"Doctor-sahib, wait, wait . . . "

I sought out Bawa-ji.

"Will you do the funeral?"

His eyes were gazing upon the mountains; he looked at me distractedly; then assented with a slow nod.

He would perform the funeral rite, with the help of Pundit Prem. The mingling of Hindu and Sikh rituals is a practice peculiar to the Punjab; the two communities are closely bound, despite those that assert otherwise.

I looked after the purchase of wood for the pyre.

A few men of the village trundled off the rough logs to the banks of the Piplan Nadi, which also served as the village cremation ground.

A rugged oblong pile was soon constructed with the wood, which was then doused with five ten-litre canisters of mustard oil bought from the general store.

It was time to bring out Raj, for his final journey.

Six of us went inside and lifted up the cot, upon which he lay. We carefully angled our way out of the door, and headed for the Piplan Nadi.

And so we bore away the corpse of the man who had once been the village teacher, the unbound traveller, the speaker of many tongues, the widower, and the true friend whom I had just begun to know.

We slowly made our way to where the Piplan Nadi flowed on, untouched by human sorrow.

When we reached the pyre, we put down the cot and lifted up the corpse.

"A man is born on a bed and is carried to his pyre on a bed . . . " an old man in the crowd observed.

Raj's body was wrapped tight in a winding sheet, with only the face exposed. We carried him around the pyre three times, moving counterclockwise, as prescribed by tradition.

Bawa-ji held the clay lamp that had earlier burned at Raj's head inside the room.

We circled the pyre, then placed the body on the heap of wood.

When we stepped back, Bawa-ji threw grains of wheat and wild flowers to sustain Raj on his eternal sojourn — the last taste of earth.

Amarnath and I then covered the body with large lumps of incense, over which we poured five buckets of clarified butter, and all the while Bawa-ji chanted a hymn from the *Rig Veda*:

Yatha anupurvam bhavanti,
Yatha rtva rtubhiryanti sadhu,
Yatha na purvamparo jahatyeva —
Dhaturayumshi kalpayaisham . . .

As day follows day,
one behind the other,
and each season trails another,
thus does a man
follow after his forefathers —
such is our life, O Lord . . .

A villager handed Bawa-ji a ladle. It was filled with fresh milk, taken from cows early in the morning when the dew still had not dried in the fields of pasture.

Bawa-ji gently pried apart Raj's lips and slowly poured the milk into his mouth; most of it dribbled away to the sides. He then placed the empty ladle away from the pyre and continued chanting the same Vedic hymn:

Lift yourself up, O earth,
and do not press down heavily upon him;
let him pass through gently.
Hold him tenderly,
as a mother wraps her own cloak
around her child.

Like the feathers of an arrow
they have laid me down
at the end of the day,
and my parting speech
I have pulled back,
as reins draw back a speeding horse.

Then Pundit Prem, slowly intoned the *Kirtan Sohila*, Guru Nanak's hymn of joy, which forms the Sikh funeral liturgy; the words speak of the bride finally meeting her beloved, her eternal spouse — the union of the soul with God; the day of the funeral was the soul's wedding day:

The day of marriage is predetermined.
Let us all gather,
and pour libations at the door.
O my friend, the departed goes
to unite with the Lord —
the news of this union

is sent to all households.
O Nanak, meditate upon Him
who sends out this news to us:
May the day of union come for us all . . .

Since there was no male relative present, Bawa-ji asked
me to light the fire; he had kindled a torch from the little
clay lamp that burned steadily on the ground.

While all watched in silence, I circled the pyre three
times, again anti-clockwise, holding the burning brand.
After the third turn, I lightly touched the torch to Raj's
forehead, and then lit the rest of the pyre.

The flames leaped and danced, as if joyous at the gift
we had prepared for them. The wood snapped brutally,
and a pall of thick, oily smoke began to form at the top
of the pyre, rising soon in a dense mass, steadily upward,
pushed higher by the flames beneath: "Bones burn like
wood; hair burns like grass . . . " Pundit Prem chanted the
words of the saint Kabir.

The wind blew cold, heralding the impending winter.
I heard no birds singing, only the apricot trees stirred and
whispered with the wind.

As the fire took hold and began to burn steadily, most
of the villagers went home.

Only a few men remained, including Bawa-ji and
Amarnath.

The pyre took two hours to burn down to a heap of
coals. It gave off a bright, crimson glow.

It was time for me to perform the final ritual. At Bawa-
ji's signal, I picked up the torch, with which I had first lit
the fire, and went to where the skull showed, white and
glowing. I let the weight of the torch gently fall upon the
burnt-through skull, nestled among the shimmering
embers like a diamond in a sea of rubies. The skull gave

a dull pop and crumbled into a heap of shards. Thus was the soul finally released from the hold of the body, rising to the vault of heaven.

And then, we all said our final farewells to Raj Kumar . . .

The funeral was now over; there was nothing further to do but let the pyre burn down to ash.

Bawa-ji and I went back to the house. He placed the lit clay lamp and a *gadvi*-pot of water where the body had lain. He then took a ritual bath to cleanse himself, as prescribed.

Once again, we found ourselves sitting outside on the cot; both of us were quiet; it was late afternoon.

"I think the villagers will perhaps get another teacher for the children," I said.

"Yes, I think they will."

Then he reached into his sack and drew out a little bundle of crimson cloth, knotted at the top.

"Raj left these things in his room. I think you should have them." Bawa-ji's hand shook slightly. "Perhaps you will know what to do with them in due time."

Untying the knot, Bawa-ji took out Raj's French passport, a slender old French-English dictionary, a little lead and silver seal depicting the Madonna, and finally the journal that I had spent my days copying — these were the brief records of a man's life; the summary of Raj Kumar's days on earth.

"Tomorrow, I shall be on my way up the mountains," Bawa-ji continued, "Will you stay on in Dhanoa?"

I said that I, too, would soon be on my way.

"Farewell, then, my young friend. A *saadh* like myself has no place to call his home. I must wander until I, too, arrive where today we left our friend Raj Kumar. I shall leave before sunrise; it's a long journey ahead — perhaps for both of us."

I arose and bowed before Bawa-ji; he got up quickly and embraced me.

"Farewell, my brother. May God lead you home." He spoke in Pashto, as he had done when we first met.

And it was as if my grandfather once again embraced me.

Bawa-ji's eyes again had that twinkle, and he gave a hearty laugh.

"They've made all these borders just to keep me out. But they don't know me. I'm going to slip through this time."

He adjusted the bundle on his back, and gripped his staff with both hands.

He stared long at the mountains.

"I want to die in Kabul."

With that he walked away.

I watched him for a long time. He passed the walnut tree and then made his way across the rope bridge, steadying himself with one hand. When he cleared the crocus fields I lost sight of him, for he swung west and passed beyond the ridge that separated Dhanoa from the mountains.

Bawa-ji did not look back. I didn't expect him to; it's considered bad luck.

He had a long trek ahead of him.

That night I was the guest of Amarnath.

Raj's house was forlorn at the edge of the village. No light burned within . . .

In the morning, Amarnath and I went to the pyre; the fire had died down, and only a few embers glowed red beneath the ash.

We gathered the ashes on a copper tray. I had with me a small brass box I had picked up in New Delhi; it had flowers engraved upon it.

I placed a small amount of ash and bone in the box from the centre of the pyre.

Then Amarnath went to the Piplan Nadi, and poured out the ashes upon the bright water, while uttering the mantra: *"Satnam, Waheguru"* ("True is the Eternal One").

I tossed some crocuses as a parting offering. The swift current bore them far away.

The body is indeed fire and water.

That same day I left Dhanoa and headed for New Delhi, from where I flew back home to Montreal.

Upon my return, I got busy with my own life, and many months passed. The little crimson bundle of Raj's belongings and the brass box that held some of his ashes lay hidden in a box in my closet, forgotten as the dead.

I HAVE FOUND THE STREETS THAT RAJ DESCRIBED, and I have walked them all, remembering my old friend, remembering Dhanoa, and my days there. And yes, the Seine does flow serenely around the city, just as he had described.

This is my second day here, and I have gotten up early, before daylight, and now I stand by the river.

I hold in my hand some roses and carnations, the brass box, and the cloth bundle that Bawa-ji gave me.

There is one last ritual left; one unfinished task.

I take the steps by the bridge honouring William the Conqueror down to the Seine. I open the brass box, which I hadn't unlocked in all these months. There he lies still, Raj Kumar. I had tried to get the ash from that spot on the burned-down pyre where I imagined his heart to be; for it was his heart that I wanted to return to Rouen; his body may have belonged to the Punjab — but his heart belonged here, in this city, in this river — a place where he found love.

I'm not a religious person, but I wish his soul peace. Then, I slowly empty the box of its contents.

There is no wind, and the ashes fall to the twilit water without scattering. I submerge the brass box in the river; it disappears in the flow.

Just then the sun shoots through the horizon, and I scatter the flowers as a final offering.

Afterwards, I go up to the Cathedral, whose doors are now open, and head inside.

I make my way up the nave towards the altar and in a side chapel dedicated to St. Bernadette, I place that crimson, knotted, cloth bundle, the earthly possessions of Raj Kumar, upon the little altar, where two steady flames burn. I leave the name and address of Marcel, which I found in Raj's journal, pinned to the bundle.

I place a few francs in the offering box and light a candle for Isabelle and another for Raj. They are together now: "May the day of union come for us all . . . "

The risen sun strikes the stained glass windows and fills the Cathedral with dappled light, arching across the vaulted ceiling and onto the flagstones.

I sit for many hours in that sacred place.

When I emerge from the Cathedral, the streets are filled with people. The air is light, and the wind from the river lifts up the many scents of summer.

There is one thing I didn't return.

I reach inside my jacket pocket; take out an envelope, and go to a nearby café.

I order a coffee, and sit and watch the crowds grow larger.

I open the envelope, and from it remove the long golden hair I found in Raj's journal.

The wind streams over me.

I raise my hand and let the hair go. I watch it float, and then it is lost to sight — finally returned after so many years.

A girl walks by me. She's very pretty; she smiles, and sits at a table nearby.

This time, my head swivels.
I smile back.
I am now a tourist.

And in this way, I accomplished my mission: I returned my friend, Raj Kumar, to Rouen, to his home, to his valley of memories, to his city of rains.